CANNIBAL FAT CAMP

MARK C. SCIONEAUX &
DAVID C. HAYES

Bizarro Pulp Press
an imprint of JournalStone Publishing

Bizarro Pulp Press
an imprint of JournalStone Publishing
Detroit⇜San Fransisco
www.BIZARROPULPPRESS.com

ISBN-13: 978-1-940161-86-0
ISBN-10: 194016186X

Printed in the USA.

Interior layout by Lori Michelle
www.theauthorsalley.com

ALSO IN THIS BOOK

CHAPTER ONE

MILES LANDISH WORKED his chubby fingers into the locker and retrieved another lunch box. Opening it, his mouth salivated at the offerings of this newest find. Escargot stuffed mushrooms, a piece of Kobe filet, and assorted truffles were all elegantly arranged for him. One of the perks of going to the most expensive school in town—all the kids brought great lunches.

He grabbed the mushrooms in his meaty paws and slammed them into his mouth. His jaws worked voraciously as he reduced them to a pulpy mush which he then swallowed down greedily. He emptied the rest of the contents down his gullet and worked on opening the next locker to retrieve its contents. He'd picked a good day, as the memo around school was the catering service that supplied school lunches was closed for the week due to an immigrant labor strike. All the kids brought food from home and Miles was in heaven. He'd been caught once already, on Monday, but now it was Friday and if he could just finish this round of gluttony, the weekend would be his, and, better yet, summer vacation was only a week away.

He popped open the next locker, which was quite

easy. All it required was a screw driver to lift up the small mechanism inside the thin-metal locker, and opened the next lunch box. He downed a thermos full of rare sheep's milk and engulfed a terrine of foie gras. Sweetbreads, with a raspberry compote, were next. The taste was too brief as the organ meat slid down his throat. Tears welled in his eyes, and he knew why. He couldn't stop. He wasn't even hungry, and, yet, here he was in the hallway after excusing himself for a bathroom break, leaving behind a wake of destruction. The tile floor was littered with lunch kits and wrappers, empty plastic containers were strewn about, tracing his path.

Beads of sweat dripped down his forehead and he felt his heart race, pumping furiously to supply sufficient blood flow to compensate for his obese stature. Miles was fat, had always been fat, and though he'd wanted to change, something inside his mind wouldn't let him. He'd diet for a day or two, even play around in the pool at home, but it would end the same—an eating binge that wiped out all the progress he'd made.

He ran a thick hand through his curly hair and mopped the sweat from his brow. The hunger subsided, and he gazed down at the mess he'd created. He had to clean it up, and fast, before Principal Hornswaggle found him. He bent down, with some effort, to pick up the thermos when he heard his pants rip. The loud tear echoed through the hall, and he became nauseous at the realization he'd forgotten to put on underwear that day. Whipping around, his foot struck a puddle of glacé and he slipped. Miles hit the ground hard, his head striking the tiled floor, and miniature stars exploded behind his eyes. He lay there in a daze, when the shrill sound of the bell announced that class was over and lunch had begun.

Oh, man. What the fuck?" He heard a male voice ask.

"Gross, I can see his balls," a female said.

"Probably the first time anyone has seen them!"

Boisterous laughter erupted through the halls, bouncing off the walls and ringing in Miles' ears. He struggled to stand up, but his hand slipped on a spilled liquid and he banged his chin. The coppery taste of blood filled his mouth, and, for once, it was something Miles didn't want to swallow.

"Ha! Look at his tiny dick!"

"I bet he's never seen it."

"Probably can't with all the fat in the way. Huh, fatty?"

"You suck Miles!"

The tears came quickly and Miles wanted to get up. The urge to beat their faces in was insurmountable, but he knew he'd just get his ass kicked. But, at least he'd have tried. His hands balled into tight fists, and he started to rise, when Principal Hornswaggle burst through the crowd.

"Damn it, Miles, not again. Get to the nurse's station right now, and then meet me in my office. This has to stop, and I'm calling your parents for a meeting immediately. The rest of you, get to lunch. Now!"

"We can't. Miles ate our lunches," a voice called out.

"Fine, just order pizzas or something and have the school billed. I don't have time to deal with this. Tell one of the teachers I said it was okay. I'm sure Miles' parents won't mind picking up the tab . . . again."

Miles hung his head in shame and made the long trek to the nurse's office. He knew it would be a long day.

***

Miles knew his dad wouldn't show up. One of the most powerful investment bankers in town, his dad had far more important things to do than occupy his time over some school lunches. He'd watched Hornswaggle's face turn beet-red and Miles knew his dad had probably laughed at the Principal and told him to just send him the bill. Unfortunately, Miles' mom—a kept woman—had nothing but free time. She was in the office right now, and Miles heard the muffled sound of voices engaged in serious conversation.

His jaw ached and his lip was sore. Luckily, the nurse supplied him with a spare set of gym shorts. He stared down at his gross, pale legs. They looked like cottage cheese stuffed inside sausage casings: lumpy, weak, and unappealing. He almost wished he was in his split pants. Flashing his balls at the entire school was kind of funny, now that he reflected on it. At least he'd left an impression before breaking for the summer.

The door to the office swung open, and Principal Hornswaggle filled the opening. An imposing man, both large in stature and size, he called to Miles in a booming voice.

"We're ready to talk with you, Miles."

Miles trudged into the office and sat down on one of the wooden chairs. His girth failed to squeeze into the seat, and piles of fat rested on the arm rest. His back ached due to the strange position he had to sit in. He looked over at his mother, who gave him a friendly smile and placed a hand on his knee. He was surprised she could smile with the amount of Botox shot up in her face.

"Oh, Miley, what are we going to do with you?" his mom asked.

Miles cringed. He hated being called *Miley*. For starters, it was a girl's name, and secondly, it wasn't even a real name. What made it worse was the name made famous by a certain Disney channel whore that he despised.

"An excellent question, Mrs. Landish," Hornswaggle said. "What do you have to say for yourself, Miles? It would be one thing if this was a one-time incident, but I've caught you now eight times this year, and that's not counting the hundreds of reports I've received from students claiming their lunches are missing. What is wrong with you?"

"I . . . I just like to eat," Miles said, sheepishly.

"Well so do I, Miles, but I have a limit. Something inside me tells me to stop eating after I'm full. You don't seem to have this."

"I'm never full. That's the problem."

"The problem, Miles, is self-control and discipline, something I feel you lack in any quantity."

"Now hold on a minute, Hornswaggle. I don't appreciate you saying things like that to my baby boy. How dare you call into question his discipline or self-control?" Miles' mother was heated.

"I apologize if that sounds harsh, Mrs. Landish, but he clearly has something wrong with him if he has to break into people's lockers to steal their food. You must agree with this behavior being abnormal."

"He's been on numerous medications and diets. Nothing seems to work. His father and I have accepted Miles for who he is. Sometimes the Lord makes us a little larger than others."

Miles' face burned with embarrassment. He looked up and noticed a jar of M&M's on Hornswaggle's desk. How he'd missed them on the way in, he'd no idea. He wanted them. Craved them. Without thinking, Miles' hand reached out and grabbed the glass container. Hornswaggle and his mother stared on, dumbstruck, as Miles emptied the entire container into his mouth. Chocolate saliva dribbled down his chin, and he chewed noisily, temporarily unaware of his surroundings.

"Well, I think my point has just been made."

"I . . . I don't know what to say," his mom said. "Miles, honey, is there something you want to tell us?"

Miles shook his head no and stared at his feet. Hornswaggle sighed and scribbled notes on a piece of paper on his desk.

"I think it would be best for everyone if Miles found a new school to go to for his senior year. Maybe even home school would be an option, but it's not working out here. Not since he started making my life difficult by stealing lunches. Do you know how many phone calls I receive a day from private chefs and parents, angry at what became of these valuable lunches?"

"I'm afraid that's just not an option," his mom said, and Hornswaggle looked as if he'd just taken a fist to the gut.

"Excuse me, Mrs. Landish, but I'm not really giving you a choice."

"Well, I am. My husband has been a huge booster of the school's football program, even though Miley isn't allowed on the team. It would pain me to tell him what happened, and for him to cancel the very large check that he has already written to you for the stadium renovations. You see, I know the other parents care more about the water polo teams and equestrian games, but football is still the money maker. In fact, why wait, I'll just text my husband now and tell him to cancel that check." She whipped out her phone and tapped on the screen.

"Hold on, Mrs. Landish. Maybe I was a bit too hasty with my judgment. We certainly wouldn't want something like that to happen."

"No, we wouldn't, would we?" She smiled.

"But something has to be done. We can't go on like this. Miles, is there anything you're not telling us? Something wrong?"

"No, not really. I'm just always hungry. I wish I could give you a reason, but even I don't know what's wrong with me. Right now I'm hungry, even though I know I'm not. It sucks," Miles said. His eyes misted.

"I have an idea. Dr. Cole, the recommended school psychiatrist and dietician, should be consulted. He's always up-to-date on the newest dieting trends. He could be invaluable for young Miles."

"Miles, honey, is that something you'd like to do? Would you want to visit with this Dr. Cole and see what he has to say?" his mom asked.

"I guess so. Not like I have much of a choice."

"Right, you don't have much of a choice," Hornswaggle said. "Believe it or not, I care about you Miles. I want to see you do well, but more importantly I want you to be healthy."

"I appreciate that, sir," Miles said.

"Then we are in agreement. Miles, meet with Dr. Cole and I'll anxiously await his diagnosis and recommendations. He will probably give you some program to work on over the summer and when you come back for your senior year, you can start a new man."

"Thank you, Principal Hornswaggle. We'll see ourselves out," Miles's mom said, and rose from her seat to shake his hand.

Miles went to stand, but realized he couldn't. His girth remained molded into the wooden chair. He panicked at the embarrassment of his situation and fidgeted. Rocking back and forth, he heard the chair creak and groan until it gave way with a mighty crack. Miles fell to the ground, rolling on his back like a lumpy turtle, his stubby appendages flailing in the air.

Principal Hornswaggle sighed as he walked over to help Miles to his feet.

CHAPTER TWO

MILES FLIPPED THROUGH magazine after magazine, waiting for his name to be called. His mom had dropped him off 30 minutes before he was due to see Dr. Cole, and he'd protested venomously. He was only two levels away from finishing his newest zombie video game when his mom shut off the television and dragged him out of the house. She had tennis lessons to go to, and their driver was occupied picking his father up from the airport. Miles had to suffer alone.

The office smelled of antiseptic and cheap tropical air freshener. The sickly sweet pineapple odor made Miles nauseous, and, for once, something food related didn't trigger a rumble in his stomach. He glanced around, taking notice of the cheap painting hanging on the wall and the frumpy, bored nurse working the desk. *Some doctor*, he thought. He wondered what was taking so long. He was the only patient waiting.

"Miles Standish," the nurse called. Her voice was gravelly and thick from years of smoking.

"It's Landish," he said, glaring.

"The doctor will see you now."

About time. Miles gripped the cool door handle and entered. A hallway lined with open doors greeted him. The nurse appeared from the side, startling him, and pointed toward a scale against the wall. She held a chart and a pen in her gnarled fingers.

"Stand flat against the wall," she ordered, and Miles placed his back on the wall next to the scale. She recorded his height.

"Five feet, nine inches. Now, on the scale."

Miles sighed, and walked over to the metal scale. He hesitated, afraid of what the number would reveal. He knew he was fat. Very fat. The scale telling him that and the nurse recording it made him feel even worse. He placed one chubby foot on the scale, and then the other. A loud, metallic *thunk!* answered back as the scale shot up.

"Looks like I need to make an adjustment," the nurse said, sliding the weights over to counter-balance Miles' girth.

Miles refused to look at the numbers. A small bead of sweat traced its way slowly down the side of his face, and he felt his heart *thud* in his chest. A wave of nausea washed over him, and, for a brief moment, he feared he may faint off the scale. He heard the nurse scribble on her paper.

"Three hundred and thirty-seven pounds," the nurse said. Miles heard nothing but condescending judgment in her voice. "And how old are you?"

"Seventeen," Miles said. He wanted to cry. Standing on the scale was turning into one of the most embarrassing moments on a long list of miserable moments.

"Well, that's a shame," the nurse said, coldly. "Go into that room," she pointed toward an open door, "and take off your shirt and sit on the bench. The doctor will be in shortly to begin the examination."

Miles said nothing. He scurried into the room,

fleeing from the prying eyes of the nurse, and closed the door. He spotted a sink and ran toward it, turning it on and using his hands as cups to gulp down water. He felt a little better as the cold water went down his throat. He rubbed his face and used a paper towel to pat it dry. The sound of the door opening behind him caused Miles to spin around . . . and lock eyes with a surprisingly pleasant face.

"Hello, Miles. My name is Dr. Cole. How are you doing today?"

"I . . . I'm fine. Nice to meet you Doctor." The doctor wasn't what he'd expected after meeting the nurse. Dr. Cole was young, and, though Miles wasn't gay, he thought the guy was quite handsome. He smiled with perfect white teeth and his steel-blue eyes made Miles feel calm and less anxious.

"Now, Miles, I know why you're here. Your principal informed me of some behavioral issues at school and he thinks your weight may play into it. I'm going to do a thorough physical exam, but also ask you some questions as well. It's been a little while, but I remember what it was like being a kid in high school. Your body is still developing, but so is your mind, and at a much quicker rate. If you ever feel uncomfortable, just let me know." He smiled.

Miles smiled back and felt his heart rate return to normal. He removed his shirt and tossed it on the chair. Dr. Cole removed his stethoscope and listened to Miles' heart and lungs. When finished, he scribbled some notes on an exam form.

"What are you writing?" Miles asked.

"Just making notes for a final report," Dr. Cole said, strapping a blood pressure monitor around Miles' flabby arm and inflating it. He recorded the number and removed the monitor. "Do you have a lot of friends, Miles?"

"No, not really. None, actually."

"What do you do for fun?"

"Mostly play video games and read. I like comic books and cooking shows. I'm a pretty good student, also."

"Yeah? Looking forward to senior year?

"Looking forward to finishing high school and going to college. Getting away from all these people and starting over."

"High school can be rough. Can you lie down, please? I want to check for any irregularities."

Miles lay down on the cold, plastic-lined bench. Dr. Cole's hands were firm and the poking and prodding hurt. Miles did his best not to show any signs of discomfort.

"What about your parents? How are they?"

"They're fine, I guess. My dad is away on business and my mom does her own thing. I usually come home to an empty house."

"That's a shame," Dr. Cole said. "Now don't be worried, but I need to do a testicular exam to check for any lumps. It's completely routine and will only take a second." The doctor placed two layers of latex gloves on his hands.

Miles almost gasped as the doctor's hands slid down his shorts and fondled his balls gently. He'd never had anyone touch them before. Miles felt saddened that the first person to lay a hand on his manhood was a doctor, and a male one at that. Dr. Cole was right, and, as quickly as he'd grabbed Miles' junk, the exam was over.

"You can put your shirt back on," Dr. Cole said, handing Miles his shirt back.

"So, how'd I do?"

"Miles, you're an intelligent young man, and I won't bullshit you. Your body is a wreck. You aren't fat, you're obese. Morbidly obese. If you keep it up this way, you might not live to 30. I know you probably get all kinds of grief for your weight, but you need to make some changes, buddy. This has nothing to do with how you look on the outside, but on the inside."

Miles sunk his head, defeated. For some reason the words coming from the doctor hurt more than the insults. The words were nothing but cold, honest truth.

"Miles, what's a typical day of eating for you?"

"I don't really know. I just eat until I don't feel like doing it anymore."

"Do you get any exercise? There has to be some activity you like that isn't video game related."

"I like to swim. Well, mostly just float around. I also like to write, but I guess that's more of a mental exercise."

"Yeah, writing is good, but don't strive to be an author. Most are over-weight alcoholics anyway." Miles let out a laugh. A brief moment of silence passed, and for reasons he didn't understand, Miles' eyes started to water. A few tears escaped and ran down his cheeks. He quickly brushed them away.

"What's wrong, Miles? Anything you tell me stays between us."

"I'm just not happy with the way I look or feel," Miles said, the tears rained down. "I feel helpless and I'm always sad, so I just eat to feel better. But I never feel better, and I keep eating because it makes me feel good for a moment, and then it goes away. I don't know what's wrong with me."

Dr. Cole placed a hand on Miles' shoulder and squeezed gently. "It's okay, buddy. I think I might have something that'll help."

Miles looked up and wiped his wet face. He expected to see Dr. Cole write out a prescription for diet pills or hand him a brochure for a new diet, but the doctor just stood there, arms crossed.

"What you need is something different. No pills. No fad diets. You need to learn how to exercise and how to eat better. You won't get that at home, but if you went away, say to a camp of some kind, you'd get the attention needed to start a better life."

"Camp? Like for the entire summer? But I was going to—"

"What? Play video games all summer? No, Miles. I need to make a call for you and for your health. Hell, you will even make new friends just like you. You'll come back for your senior year a brand-new, but more importantly, healthier man, ready to take on the world."

"I don't have much of a choice, do I?"

"Afraid not. The school, and your parents, have left it up to my medical opinion. Study hard when you get to college, Miles, and be a doctor. We get to do all kinds of fun stuff."

"And make a ton of money," Miles said.

"Well that, too, but to be honest, you aren't exactly hurting, nor will you ever. So just imagine that. You'll have the money and a new body. Those girls in college will be all over you. So what do you say? Are you going to give camp a shot?"

"Like you said, I don't have much of a choice."

"Good enough for me." Dr. Cole held out his hand and Miles took it. The doctor had a firm handshake, and though Miles squeezed back, he was no match.

"I'm going to shake your hand when you get back, too. Good luck, Miles. The nurse will check you out."

***

*Medical professional, please do not forget to indicate your *Camp Tum Tum Preferred Provider Number* during form submission to ensure prompt commission remittance after tuition payments have cleared.

Your Camp Tum Tum Account Representative is: Margaret Nelson, x.76566
Referring Physician Name: Mason Cole, M.D.
PPN: 636545

CAMP TUM TUM
PHYSICAL EXAMINATION FORM, v.2

Name: Miles Landish
School: Robert Dole High School
Date of Birth: 11/22/1995
School Year: Junior
Student I.D.#: A11260390
S.S.#: 556-98-9632
Local Address: See attached file
Phone#: See attached file

Please list the dates for these vaccinations:
MMR 1: 1990s, ish
Polio primary series completed: 1990s
Tuberculosis Test: LOL
Hepatitis B series completed: N/A
Last Tetanus Booster: _____

List any medications patient is currently taking (this includes over the counter supplements, birth control, etc.):

He's probably eaten his mother's 'prescription' Xanax. It looks like Tic Tacs.

Allergies:

Exercise, willpower (Margaret: remind me to tell you a joke I heard about a fat kid, canola oil and flour).

Check and record date of any illness/condition you have or had in the last 5 years:

Arthritis: Soon
Frost Bite: Won't go outside
Heat Illness: From Video Games?
Asthma: No Hay Fever: No
Surgery: Future lipo candidate!
Concussions: NO
Mononucleosis: The kissing disease? Ha!
Hospitalization: Soon
Diabetes: Don't ask
Heart Problems: Tomorrow
Tuberculosis: No
Epilepsy: No
Rheumatic Fever: No

Explain any current illness and/or medical limitations:

Current medical limitations include, but are not limited to: laziness, overindulgent parents, lack of discipline and inability to see toes when standing. Ha! Hey, when you're in town again want to get some dinner? That Tum Tum expense account needs to get a work out as much as this kid. Page me.

Do any of the following apply to the patient?:

Y **High Blood Pressure**
N **Use of Orthotics**
N **Scoliosis**
Y **Heart Problems**
N **Wear Contacts/glasses**
Y **Unpaired Organ (i.e. 1 kidney)**
N **Seizures**
N **Migraines**
N **Asthma**
Y **Hearing Aid**
Y **Other ____**

Explain any YES answers:

Miles is morbidly obese, like that is any surprise. He will develop high blood pressure and heart problems; that is inevitable. He has trouble hearing because the kid is chewing all the time . . . all the time. His principal told me that the fat bastard has been breaking into other kids' lockers and eating their lunches. It's compulsive! There wasn't a check box to indicate that he has "Double Organs" (i.e. 2 stomachs). LOL. I slay me. You miss my jokes, admit it.

N **Passed out during sports**

Unless speed eating is a new sport, this kid has absolutely no threat of passing out during physical activity. In all reality, the camp would be good for him. Might keep him alive long enough to cash in on that huge trust fund. Remind me if referring physicians are still entitled to multi-year bonuses. This Landish kid looks like eight pounds of potatoes in a five pound sack. He's a two summer project, easy.

N **Family history of death before 50**

From what the school tells me the parents and family are normal sized so this is all psychological. Counseling and therapy will be necessary while in-camp just to keep the kid on the program. He'd probably try and kill himself if he wasn't so lazy. Strike that, his life is one giant suicide attempt right now.

Y **Irregular periods?**

Although patient is male, he whines like it's a heavy flow day. He's an emotional eater so, of course, Daddy isn't around bullshit is the cause célèbre. When you get out this way, we should try this new sushi place. You know, share a couple of rolls?

MEDICAL EXAMINATION
Instructions: Examiner, after completing the previous section, record your comprehensive examination here. This will determine the examinee's fitness for the Camp Tum Tum experience. Please be honest and indicate areas where the examinee may need additional help and exactly why the examinee may or may not be a good fit for Camp Tum Tum. These standards are very strict and we only wish to provide examinees that have a good chance of success at camp. In addition, do not forget to submit a declaration of examinee's known financial situation, if available. If the examinee has a fitness determination that does not indicate that he or she would make a viable Tum Tum candidate, please indicate to examinee behaviors that may increase his or her chances upon the next visit. If there are special considerations to be taken into account, the examiner is responsible for documenting such.

Height 5' 9" **Weight** 337#
Blood Pressure 160/100
Temperature 98.9 **Pulse** DNR

EXAMINATION
1. **Skin** Pale, splotchy. Areas of skin that are reachable are clean and psoriasis-free. Other areas have large, heat-related rash areas (underneath breasts, thighs, underarms, etc.).
2. **Head, face and scalp** Generally clear of issues. Poor diet is affecting baldness already.

3. **Ears, tympanic membranes** Fine.
4. **Eyes, pupils, fundi, motion** On "see" food diet. Get it?
5. **Nose, sinuses, olfaction** Can smell a cookie in upwards of fifty feet away upwind. I promise to stop joking when you get here . . . sushi!
6. **Mouth, throat, speech** Mouth and throat are incredibly strong.
7. **Neck, thyroid** Unknown. Couldn't find his neck . . . sorry, couldn't stop.
8. **Heart** Prognosis doesn't look good
9. **Varicosities, bruits, pulses** Circulation is slow in general through a sedentary lifestyle (self-reported video game junkie).
10. **Chest, lungs** The ironic part is that his man flaps look like lungs on the outside of his body. No joke.
11. **Breasts** (if indicated) Yeah.
12. **Abdomen, hernia** No, and I'm still trying to get the smell off my hand. I don't know how, but even his scrotum smelled like chili.
13. **Rectum** (if indicated) N/A. Maybe next time. Maybe not.
14. **Endocrine** N/A.
15. **Spinal mobility, alignment** Compromised.
16. **Upper extremities, hands** I swear to you, Margaret, his knuckles looked like little Sharpei puppy faces.

17. **Lower extremities, feet** Ever seen Lord of the Rings?
18. **Muscle strength, tone** Able to move over three hundred pounds from couch to toilet multiple times per day.
19. **Gait, Rhomberg** Shrek-like.
20. **Balance, coordination** N/A.
21. **Reflexes** N/A.
22. **Cranial Nerves** N/A.
23. **Mental Status** Bleak. Like I've said, Miles is wrapped up in "Daddy didn't love me" mode so he eats to compensate for that. He is a whiner and I thought the kids was going to start crying right there. He is a PRIME candidate for the program and I've made the prescription.

Signature of examining health care provider
[signed]
Date: May 4, 2012
Print name of examining health care provider: Dr. Mason Cole, M. D.

INSTRUCTIONS: Examiner, this section should be utilized to summarize any additional medical history, abnormal physical findings, diagnostics, lab results, etc. Also, please feel free to give your opinion regarding fitness for camp and the possibility of tangible success. In addition, please relate any social knowledge you have of the examinee so we can target that. We need to be clear: whether or not the examinee is accepted into the program, and whether or not your commission is approved, is many times decided in this section. Sufficient documentation is absolutely necessary and helps our Tum Tum Outreach Team in the first contact with the examinee.

In the event that the examinee is found unfit for Tum Tum, we ask that you request a behavior modification form from your Account Representative detailing the recommendations you will make to the examinee in order to, hopefully, affect a positive outcome during the next examination. Use additional sheets if necessary.

NOTES:

Miles Landish is a morbidly obese seventeen-year-old, as we have already established. I do not believe it is a biological condition (like something related to the pituitary gland or thyroid), he just eats. He eats a lot. He has psychosomatically convinced himself that eating is pleasurable and it has taken the place of real parenting. His father, from what I gleaned from Miles, is rarely around. Miles' principal indicates that his mother is the only point of contact and that the father is deep into hedge fund management. Judging by the zip code, and my conversation with Miles, financially and emotionally he is ready for Tum Tum.

I do have a couple of questions

regarding his willpower, including his reasoning for wanting to lose weight. From what I could gather, his school life is miserable and the poor bastard is a virgin. (This may be TMI, but he actually started to stiffen up when I gave him the hernia check. I nearly lost it there . . . now you definitely owe me sushi!) If possible, I had some success using potential mates and he responded enthusiastically when the prospect of 'girls falling over him' was mentioned. This is where the conversation needs to lead. Stealing lunches is one thing but teenage hormones bouncing around a body that big is a different matter entirely.

Miles' mother refused to admit there is a problem. She seems to want whatever Principal Hornswaggle indicates and I've submitted my recommendation to him as well. As I've indicated, this candidate is PRIME and should be recruited immediately.

Now, about that dinner . . . call me.

Signature of examining health care provider
[signed]
Date May 4, 2012
Printed name of examining health care provider Dr. Mason Cole, M.D.

CHAPTER THREE

FOR IMMEDIATE RELEASE
Los Angeles, CA—CAMP TUM TUM OPENS DOORS WIDE FOR CAMPERS!

Don't think of it as a fat camp, think of it as a balanced dietary and fitness home away from home . . . on a beautiful tropical island! Welcome to Camp Tum Tum, a temptation deprivation and isolation oasis for overweight teens.

Now, don't think of it as a 'fat camp.' Fat camps are filled with desperate, morbidly obese children that have been taken from their grief-stricken guardians in the middle of the night. Their plump, greasy bodies are tossed in a panel van and then transported, against their will, to some second rate renovated campground that the Catholic church probably had to give up because of litigation.

Not Camp Tum Tum.

Where the 'fat camp' would only serve the most disgusting gruel available and force the pudgy campers to undergo hardships used to train Russian soldiers, the experience would ultimately result in resentment, fear and loathing. All three of these things are catalysts to overeating.

Not Camp Tum Tum.

Too much of this world is devoted to placing a premium on what our outside looks like and very little worth is placed on what our insides look like. At Camp Tum Tum, we prefer a whole big body approach. We call it "Wholistic Weight Loss" and it is a proven winner. When campers arrive at Camp Tum Tum, their insides are nothing more than globs and globs of fleshy black fat. It is runny and smells like something they ate wasn't dead yet. This is both literal and figurative. The poor, morbidly obese children that labor over our doorstep are physically and emotionally rotting from the inside out. That is where we come in.

Camp Tum Tum is most definitely not the traditional fat camp. We provide nutritious, balanced meals that taste great. Our award-winning chefs have studied around the globe in order to prepare the finest cuisine available. Our staff, who we are proud to call our "Weight Artists" have all competed in at least one Olympic Games and are at the pinnacle of physical and mental capacity for their age (and don't worry, we don't allow Winter Olympics competitors to work at Camp Tum Tum). Our staff ensures that your child will be receiving the highest quality of care and encouragement as well as nutrition and fitness coaching.

Most of all, Camp Tum Tum is free of all temptations. All parents and guardians are required to sign a temporary release of guardianship. The location of the tropical island used for Camp Tum Tum activities is secret . . . no one must know. Contact with campers will be at a minimum. This is to ensure that there are no outside distractions. Weight loss is serious business. Cell phones and computer devices are strictly forbidden, and this applies to campers as well as staff! There is only one satellite phone on the entire island in case of emergencies and it is under lock and key. There must be absolutely NO contact with the outside world. The outside world is where fatty foods and sedentary lifestyles live. Not at Camp Tum Tum!

But Camp Tum Tum is fun! Campers will finally be in a social setting where they don't have to feel embarrassed to be exactly who they are. Over the course of the twelve-week program (fitting nicely into that summer break from school), the campers will learn, love and grow with one another (not physically, mind you) as they shed those flabby pounds and relieve all the stress on their hearts in order not to have a stroke or heart attack before they enter the prime of their lives. Too many times have we seen large, lumbering teens completely reject their own futures and become wrapped up in that spiral of food addiction, laziness and diabetic amputations. As we like to say at Camp Tum Tum . . . not on our watch!

Most importantly, Camp Tum Tum is a judgment-free environment. Even though some of our campers have come to Camp Tum Tum without the basic skills needed to survive, we have open arms here. Whether or not rectum cleanliness is possible due to the threat of dislocating a shoulder or only one tooth proudly hangs from gums that look like licorice, the Camp Tum Tum staff is ready, and willing, to accept one and all without judgment. We know how hard it is to stop the cycle of addiction. Food addiction. We know that the effort it takes to clean underneath one’s pendulous breasts or catch every bit of organic matter that may settle in sweaty crevasses and grow . . . we know. Rest assured, even the most disease-ridden youth can find solace here. Will they be judged?

Not at Camp Tum Tum.

What everyone realizes soon enough is that we are all in this together. No contact with the hateful outside world means that we can only rely on one another and ourselves. What every Camp Tum Tum camper will realize boils down to a simple truth: everyone here is in the same boat. They haven't been shipped off to any old fat camp; they've been shipped off to a land of real liberty, a land of choices and consequences that make sense. They have come to Camp Tum Tum to become better people of their own free will and that is the difference.

This is what we know: A morbidly obese teen is an unhappy teen that probably only avoids suicide because the physical effort is simply too great. Being a teenager of average size is difficult, but an overweight teen is positively miserable. He or she has no one, really. Parents run the gamut from blinding themselves to the problem at hand or being part of the problem and enabling these young people to stuff their faces.

The worst part comes in the form of other teenagers. Name calling, physical abuse and emotional terrorism are inevitable. Some obese teens manage to develop coping mechanisms. Others shovel Twinkies® in their mouths in an effort to fill that gaping emotional void. It won't work. Only the skill set that comes with a session at Camp Tum Tum can stop that avalanche of fried and battered depression from dropping on the youth of America.

Finally, parents and guardians can rest assured that their precious cargo, their children, will not be forced by some kind of liberal agenda to co-mingle with rabble. Everyday street kids with weight problems simply cannot afford the tuition at Camp Tum Tum. The level of service that we provide is second to none. Consider your most valuable assets safe and secure and far, far away from prying eyes. And, of course, the stature that you parents have earned in the community will never, ever be sullied through an affiliation with Camp Tum Tum. We are discreet and, if we may be so bold, some of our clients have had a Presidential disposition . . . so rest assured. We will turn that obese secret you've been hiding into a valuable member of your family and a future you can be comfortable investing in.

For more information about Camp Tum Tum and our staff, please feel free to call 1-877-CAMPTUM. There you will speak directly to one of our Castaway Counselors and be given an SSL secured website, username and password after the obligatory background check.

The answer to all your problems is only a phone call away.

CHAPTER FOUR

MILES CRACKED OPEN another can of diet soda and chugged it down in three long gulps. Tossing the can aside, he picked up another and dug his hands into a big bag of pork rinds. The pork snacks were salty and crisp, and, the more he chewed, the better he felt. His fingers worked overtime on the grease stained video game remote control. Zombie heads burst in beautiful colors of reds and purples on the 80" television that was mounted to his wall. With every head shot, he thought about Dr. Cole.

When he'd left the doctor's office, he'd felt better. In fact, it was the best he'd felt in ages. He'd jumped in the pool that day and swam a few laps, nothing strenuous, but one had to start somewhere. That night, he'd passed on his usual pizza and French fries and had the chef fix him some steamed broccoli with a chicken breast. The chef laughed hard at the request, assuming it was a joke. When it wasn't, the professionally trained cook fired up the grill, and cooked Miles a meal that even he had to admit was pretty good for diet food. *This isn't so bad*, he had thought. *I can do this!*

As the days passed, so did Miles' willpower. He cheated a little each day on his diet until there was little left that resembled a diet of any kind. Defeated, he gave up, and returned to his video games. There his characters were thin and good looking. They had hard bodies and were able to scale mountains while firing heavy weapons and fucking slutty, pixilated chicks. He dreamed of being one of them. He knew the representative for the camp would come any day now, and, as the days went, he wondered if they would come at all. Perhaps the doctor had been wrong and changed his mind. Maybe Miles wasn't a good candidate at all for the rigors of this fat camp for the elite.

He tossed the empty bags of pork skins on the floor and grabbed a cylinder of potato crisps. The can opened with a satisfying pop and Miles downed the contents greedily. He wiped the BBQ flavored dust off his face and licked his fingers clean. Letting out a large belch, he returned to his dream world: being the savior of a world gone to Hell in the middle of a zombie apocalypse.

"Miles?" The door to his bedroom creaked open and his father stepped in.

Troy Landish was a tall, powerful man. When he walked into a room, he owned it, and people flocked to him. Jet black hair, a strong jaw, and powerful shoulders, Troy was a winner in life. Looking at the fat slob his son had turned into hurt his heart. He blamed himself for Miles' failures, knowing he was always away on business and couldn't devote any time to raising his son. His wife was worthless, merely a piece of eye-candy for important dinners and social events. All the women in this zip code were. Miles glanced over, surprised that his father actually entered his room.

"Dad? Hey. It's been a while. How was China?"

"Oh, you know, son, same as always. When you've been so many times, the luster wears off."

"Yeah, I'm sure," Miles said. His dad never offered to take him to China.

"How you doing, Miles? You been all right?"

Miles felt like crying. *Just take a look at me! Do I look all right?* He wanted to scream. "I'm fine, Dad. Saving the world by killing one zombie at a time."

"That's great, son. Really . . . great." His voice trailed and he cleared his throat. "Your mother and I would like you to come downstairs. There is someone here who wants to talk to us, especially you."

"The camp guy, huh? I was wondering when he'd show."

"Yep, it's him. How about you clean up a little and then head downstairs? He seems like a really nice guy. We've been chatting with him for a little while now, getting to know him a bit, and he's really dedicated his life to helping kids get healthy."

Miles knew there was no point arguing with his dad. He was surprised at his father's approach, actually, as the old man typically barked orders. He was surprisingly calm and subdued. Miles felt on edge.

"Sure, Dad. I'll be right down."

"Thanks, son." He smiled and closed the door.

Miles walked into the private bathroom and washed his face, removing the layer of grease from around his mouth. He ran a comb through his hair and put on a fresh t-shirt, one without stains. A spritz of cologne followed and Miles was trudging down the spiral staircase to the floor below.

He entered the living room, and saw his parents

seated on the sofa speaking with a man that Miles thought looked to be carved from a block of obsidian. His bald head shone from the overhead light and his skin was as dark as the darkest chocolate that Miles could imagine. The man smiled and revealed a row of perfectly straight, white teeth. He strode forward on powerful legs and his arms rippled with muscles. His shirt was tight around his stomach, and Miles could see each abdominal muscle flex and release with every step. The man towered over him and offered his hand. Miles took it, limply, and yelped as the man crushed the chubby mitt in his grip.

"Hello, Miles. My name is Julius, your Camp Tum Tum welcome counselor."

"Hi, Julius," Miles said, flexing his hand back and forth. He worried if this would affect his video game abilities.

"Go have a seat on the couch with your parents," Julius said. The man's voice was booming with confidence. "I have something I want to show you all."

Miles walked over and plopped down in-between his mom and dad. His mom moved in closer and put an arm around him. His dad pushed away, giving him space. Julius walked in front of the family and stood posed like a statue.

"Take a good look at me, Miles. You see all this? The muscles? The confidence? The posture? What if I told you that when I was your age, I looked like you?"

"I'd say you're full of shit," Miles said.

"Miles! Manners," his mom said.

"No, it's okay. I can't blame you for thinking that. But it's true. Here, I'll show you."

Julius pressed a button on the TV remote and the

screen came to life. What was displayed shocked Miles. It looked like a juvenile version of Julius, but instead of the sculpted muscles, globs of fat flowed down his body. He looked miserable, and Miles knew that pained look on his face all too well.

"How . . . I mean, how did you—?"

"How do I look like this now? Well I'll tell you it wasn't easy. See, Miles, I wasn't lucky like you to have parents who could provide me with things. I grew up in the hood. When my momma cooked dinner, it was the cheapest, most unhealthy stuff you could find. I'm surprised I didn't drop dead. But one day, after getting beat up for the hundredth time, I said 'Julius, it's time you made a change.' And that's what I did."

"What'd you do?" Miles was on the edge of his seat.

"I started running, eating better, and lifting weights. I'd go to the junkyard by my house and lift pieces of iron and steel until I could barely lift my arms. I'd find the dog that guarded the place, a nasty, mean-ass pit bull called Bruce-Bruce, kick him in the ass and then run like hell. Sometimes I got away, other times, he got me."

Julius shoved his forearm in Miles' face and he gasped at the horrific scar caused by the bite of a powerful and pissed off dog.

"But I never gave up. The day came when that dog couldn't even keep up with me. I was a new man. I was healthy and it felt great. I got out of that ghetto. I did well in school and studied health and nutrition in college. My passion has been helping kids like me. There are so many who feel they have no hope. That they will never get healthy, but believe me, Miles, if you want it bad enough, you can achieve it."

"But what if I don't have what you have? I don't have the willpower, Julius."

"Well that's why I'm here, to push you along the way. At Camp Tum Tum, you aren't alone in your struggles. You'll be surrounded with people trying to lose weight. They will be some of the most inspiring ones you'll meet. In addition, counselors like me will be there to always help. We're available for extra sessions, or just to sit down and have a talk. Now, I know you've seen the movies about fat camps and they look like big jokes, but, trust me, this isn't one of those camps. It is so exclusive, that no one even knows you'll be there, other than mom and dad, of course."

Miles' mom smiled and his dad let out a soft chuckle.

"I have so many questions," Miles said.

"Here, let me play the video for you. It will explain everything. It's not long, because that kind of stuff is boring." Julius pressed another button on the remote and the movie started.

"In high definition Blu-ray," Julius said. "The owners spare no expense."

Miles sat, transfixed by the screen. It opened with a massive helicopter setting down gently on a lush, tropical island. Emerald water and gorgeous waterfalls set a breathtaking view. Palm trees stood tall along sugar white beaches. It was truly paradise.

"Pretty sweet, huh?" Julius said. "We hold work out sessions on the beach to let you kids enjoy the outdoors. You'll find working out more enjoyable when it's in a nicer setting than in a gym."

The video continued, and a row of chubby kids lined up. A cut sequence showed various exercises and weigh-ins. Kids sat in a lavish dining hall that resembled a fine dining restaurant. They dined on roasted meats and fresh vegetables. The food looked exquisite.

"Not gonna lie to you, my man. The food is delicious and healthy. You'll learn a lot about what you should be eating and what you should avoid. But it's not all strict. We do have an ice cream night and a pancake breakfast. There are some rewards, but when eaten in moderation, those foods aren't all that bad."

Miles watched as the campers lounged about by large pools and received massages from good-looking staff members. Hard-bodied women stood as sentinels around the aqua lounge, making sure all campers were tended to.

"I don't need to tell you that the women are very nice to look at," Julius said, smiling.

The video concluded with a before and after of each camper, and Miles was shocked. Some kids had lost over a hundred pounds and the looks on their faces were priceless. Miles wanted that look. It was one of hope and contentment. Not from eating a big meal, either, but knowing they were finally in control of their own lives. He needed that.

"When can I go?" Miles asked.

"Well hold on now, sport," his dad interjected. "Mr. Julius, this looks very impressive, and expensive, but how are we assured this is all in Miles' best interest. Is there some kind of guarantee this works?"

"Mr. Landish, when a camper comes to Camp Tum Tum, he is weighed and a goal is set based on the pre-screening physical. If the camper doesn't lose half the weight we said he would then a full refund is given. Failure isn't an option at Camp Tum Tum."

"Well, I guess that's good to know. Not that money is an issue, but shit, I could send the kid around the world for the cost of this summer camp."

"Don't think of it like a vacation. Think of it as investing in your son's health. Miles will be given all the tools and knowledge to succeed not only at Camp Tum Tum, but also in life. I wish I had the opportunity you can afford for him, but I wasn't blessed with such means."

Troy glanced over at Miles, who was transfixed on the film credits, which featured attractive female lifeguards splashing in the pool. He wished for a moment he was going.

"When can I go?" Miles asked, again. He was annoyed his previous question had been interrupted.

"The helicopter leaves in three days. You'll have enough time to eat all your favorite foods and do whatever you want before devoting your time and energy into the Camp Tum Tum lifestyle."

"How long are they gone for?" Miles' mom asked.

"It's a ten-week program. They are required to write a letter and a journal entry every night for their own mental wellbeing. It's fascinating what the human mind comes up with when introduced to a situation it's not accustomed to."

"Well then, Mr. Julius, I think this all sounds good." Troy offered his hand and Julius shook it firmly. "Miles, what do you feel like eating tonight?"

"Everything," Miles said, and smiled.

***

The chopper blades swirled violently and the winds caused Miles' cheek fat to ripple. He stood on the helipad with his parents, and a dozen kids just like him and their parents. His mom hadn't stopped crying, and Miles didn't understand why. It's not like she'd even know he was gone after she enjoyed a five martini lunch and an afternoon at the spa. But, she was at least making an effort, and Miles kind of loved her for that. His dad was busy mingling with the other powerful and elite members of society. For as rich as these men were, they were all saddled by the same affliction: their children were out of control hogs.

"Oh, Miley," his mom dabbed her eyes, "I'm so sorry I let you get this way." She was bawling now.

"Mom, it's okay. I'm going to get better. It's not your fault. You didn't make me eat all the time." He hugged her and she hugged back.

"Attention everyone!" Julius emerged from the large, military-style chopper. "We will be boarding soon. Please say your goodbyes now, and then kids, hand me your boarding pass and climb aboard."

Hugs and kisses were exchanged, and more than a few tears were shed. Miles and the others formed a single-file line and slowly plodded to the helicopter. He handed his pass to Julius, who gave him a big smile. Miles climbed the stairs, winded after finishing the five-step climb, and found his seat. He looked around, and wondered if the chopper would be able to take off with a dozen kids like him weighing it down. The doors closed and Julius walked past the future campers, taking his seat next to the pilot.

There was a feeling of weightlessness as the engines roared and chopper lifted off the ground. Miles stared down and saw his family waving. From the elevation he was at they appeared tiny, and Miles sat back and closed his eyes. It would take three hours to reach the island; he wanted to be well-rested for when he started his new life.

CHAPTER FIVE

Mandatory Letter Home, Day One: Landish, Miles

Hello mother, hello father,

I don't know if I can do this anymore. I mean, I know it's the first day and I know that we're required to do these letters for you guys, but I don't know. I want to change, I really do. I really, really want to change. I'm just not sure that I can do it.

Getting here was the easy part. The helicopter ride was cool, a little bumpy, but it was my first time on a real one. It started great, I felt kind of normal. There are a ton of other kids here and they look just like me. Some were a little bigger, some were a little smaller but we all had issues. We could just look each other in the eye and we just knew, you know? We just knew that we were all here for the same purpose. It was great and, for once, I belonged somewhere. Then it fell apart. For all of us.

Part of me really hates that you sent me here. The other part blames myself for getting so excited to want to come here. What gets me very, very angry right now is knowing you don't care. I know you think you're doing the right thing and that it's easier to just forget about me and throw me on some island and hopefully turn me into the son you wanted me to be, but it's just not working out like that. It's the first day and I can't look at myself in the mirror without feeling ashamed. Maybe that's the whole point of this, I don't know. But it hardly seems right that I should be feeling that way.

When we got to the island the first goal we had was to carry our luggage about forever to our cabin. Julius said it was only a mile but I don't know, it just was so hard and it should've been easy. It was very disappointing that I felt I couldn't finish the mundane task of walking a certain distance. And the luggage had wheels on it! The cabin is nice, though, and my roommate is cool. I'm staying with a guy named Charles York. He's from Boston and is about my size, maybe a little taller. Same width, actually. We joked about that. Apparently, Charles' family made a bunch of money during prohibition in the 1920s and his parents don't really work. They kind of fly around all over the place and leave him on his own. Sound familiar? Maybe I understand why I'm here a little better than you think I do.

Anyway, it took us forever to just catch our breath after walking to the cabin. We unpacked and saw that the cabin had nice beds, comfortable, and at the same time we both saw the schedule posted on the wall next to the bathroom door. This place is no joke and not very much like the video Julius showed us. I feel ripped off. You should feel ripped off, but I know you don't. It's just one drop in the bucket when it comes to money with you both. Here, this is what the daily schedule looks like:

0600 Rise and shine
0620 Morning calisthenics (before we even eat!)
0645 Breakfast (and if breakfast is anything like the dinner we had this really won't work)
0715 Daily pep rally
0800 Island hike (they said it would be like three miles . . . every day!)
1000 Water training (this may not be so bad)
1200 Lunch
1230 Aerobics (seriously . . . with nylon shorts and stuff)
1300 Group sessions (I do have Charles in my group, so that's cool, I guess)
1430 Free time
1700 Dinner
1800 Nature walk (another hike, seriously!)
1930 Social interaction (it really says that, forced discussion is more like it)
2100 Mandatory hygiene
2130 Lights out

That's the schedule every day. Every day! The exercise alone is enough to kill someone. I bet trained athletes can't handle this kind of activity every day. Two hikes? Calisthenics? I even had to ask Charles how to spell it.

And they took away my phone. I knew we weren't going to have any contact with the mainland, or you guys, or our lives back home, but to take away our phones? I don't know why, but I thought I'd get a chance to, you know, maybe even play a videogame on my phone or check Facebook or something . . . but I guess not. That two and half hours of free time really don't mean much, now do they?

And I feel empty.

I remember what I ate before we went to the airport. The polish sausage and sauerkraut were awesome, but as soon as we were airborne, the hunger returned. Luckily, dinner was served in an hour, after we checked into our rooms. I was excited until I saw what dinner was. Dinner consisted of one plain chicken breast, a cup of broccoli (no butter, of course), a half of a sweet potato (which tasted like flavorless mush) and water. All the water I could drink. They made us start the meal off with two glasses of water, and end it with another two. I feel hollow, empty, like a big black hole. My stomach is making weird noises. I know when I had Chef make this stuff it was really good and this food didn't taste bad, there just was nothing to it. Nothing. I don't know if I'm going to make it. I already feel like I'm starving. I know I'm not and it's just my mind and my food addiction but I want to cry. Too bad if that isn't manly enough. It's how I feel.

It looks like everyone is equally as miserable as I am. I don't understand how anyone can get used to this. Why can't people just accept me for who I am? Am I a bad person? I'm so sorry about the other kid's lunches and I promise I will never do it again, but please let me come home. Please.

Julius came by the cabin to see how Charles and I were doing. I couldn't help it, I begged him to let me go home. So did Charles! Julius just laughed. He said, "Every camper that's ever come to Camp Tum Tum has said the same thing on the first night. You'll thank me when this is over." And then he left. He just turned around and left. I don't know what to do. Even with Charles, I feel more alone than usual.

As you can probably imagine, not many people talk during dinner. It's not like the room was full of highly social people. I sat next to Charles because we'd already met, but still, socially awkward fat kids aren't the best conversationalists. And when we saw what dinner was made of that just added to the depression in the room.

The counselors sit by themselves on the opposite side of the cafeteria. Each one of them is beautiful. Their bodies are perfect, their smiles are perfect, and they laughed and talked with each other through the entire meal. Except for the sound of chewing, the staff table made all the noise in the room. And they didn't eat! Not one of them ate real food. Each one of the staffers, in their bright neon orange Camp Tum Tum staff shirts, drank a large protein shake. Before dinner was served they explained exactly what they were about to consume. It was a shake made in the blender that consisted of a protein powder supplement for working out, fresh fruits, and dehydrated peanut butter blended with water and ice. They even said on some nights we'd just have the shakes for dinner. If there had been anything in my stomach at that point, I would've barfed. And that was that. They drank their shakes, laughed and had a great time. We ate broccoli and then shuffled back to the cabin to finish unpacking. I hate it here.

I've come to a couple of realizations since I've been here, and it's only taken a few hours. I'm nothing like you expected me to be, I get that. I'm a disappointment. I realize now that as much as I want to change I just don't have the determination or the willpower to change. It's too difficult. I'm sorry dad, I know you expected more. But, maybe I expected more as well. Maybe I do deserve to be here.

I know why I'm here. It's easier to forget about me when I'm on some island and not standing there, disgusting you just by existing. I have problems but they could be worse, right? Maybe all I really needed was for you to be a little more interested in me. I eat because I'm lonely. I finally realized that. And even here, surrounded by people just like me, I'm still lonely.

We'll see what tomorrow brings.

Sincerely,
Miles

CHAPTER SIX

From the *San Antonio Times*:

Man Suspected of Poisoning Protein Powder Takes Own Life

Mexico City, Mexico—A man accused of intentionally contaminating thousands of pounds of the new protein powder MEGA SWOLE was found dead today in his cell as he waited trial for murder. Horatio Chavez, 49, a line worker for Total Fitness Corporation at their Mexico City headquarters, stood accused of lacing batches of the chocolate-flavored supplement with ricin in what was a possible revenge tactic.

Total Fitness Corporation has issued an immediate cessation of all sales of its products and ordered their entire line of workout supplements to be recalled. Currently, no products are being made at any of the corporation's facilities, which span across the globe. The loss of profits and the mounting death toll may spell the end for the supplement giant. Total Fitness Public Relations director, Miranda Schwartz, only released the following statement via Twitter, reading, "TFC is saddened by news will investigate. BRB with more."

Chavez, whose wife filed for divorce and remarried a manager at the plant where he was employed, died in his jail cell. He used his prison-issued shirt to form a noose for which was utilized to hang himself. Total Fitness Corporation agents have been dispersed to all regions where their products are sold in an effort to ensure all products are returned and to smooth over talks that their entire line is tainted. Neither Chavez's ex-wife nor the plant manager could be reached for comment.

At time of publication, the death toll stands at 27 people, with more expected as news travels of the deadly powder.

***

"You ever snort a line of protein powder? Shit burns like hell."

Julius dumped a container of chocolate protein powder on the table. Using his hands, he formed a jagged line and removed a straw from his pocket. He snorted and the line disappeared. His eyes glazed for a moment, and he coughed a dusty cloud of cocoa. The entire room went nuts.

"Oh shit, man. I can't believe you did that,"

Maxwell Powers, the head cardio coach, said, slapping him on the back.

"Learn something new at all these camps," Wendy Latrine said. "As an aerobics instructor, I'm more into carbs than into protein."

"Well that's because you're a lesbian. You could use a good shot of protein every now and then," Collin Lamb said, darting out his tongue and laughing.

"Right, like the aqua aerobics instructor would know anything about a vagina."

"Except resembling one," Boris Nakitoff said. The large, muscle-bound giant let out a hearty laugh, and the others followed suit.

"This is our last night of fun people," Julius said. "Tomorrow we get to work molding these fat, sad lumps into something semi-respectable. You have any vices you want to get out your system, do it tonight. Need to fuck? Get it out of the way? Have any drugs or alcohol on you? Consume it all. After tonight, we get serious."

"You're such a fucking buzzkill, Jules," Collin said. He drank down his protein shake and opened the tub to make another. It was empty.

"Goddamit, Boris. You fucking Nazi mutant. You already went through the entire tub of powder. It hasn't even been a day."

"Boris is not German, he is proud Russian. And he will crush your skull if you call him that again." The large man puffed his chest out and his cold, blue eyes stared down the retreating Collin.

"Sorry, man. My bad. Guess I'll go scrounge up some more." He got up and went to find another tub of protein powder.

"Make sure you grab some peanut butter and

coconut milk. Figure we'll all have one last celebratory shake before tomorrow. Hey, you all back there. Come sit up with us."

Julius motioned to the six young intern trainers sitting in the back. All in school for health and nutrition, the college-aged pack scrambled to join their peers. They were earning valuable credit for serving at the camp, and wanted to learn all they could from the best.

"Sir, thank you for—" one, a male, started to say before Julius cut him off.

"Kid, I didn't say you could talk. Shut up and just be here, okay?"

The older trainers snickered. Maxwell ogled a shapely female who gave him the stink-eye. Collin emerged from the back, holding a 30 pound drum of Mega Swole Chocolate-Flavored Protein Powder.

"Ugh, chocolate again?" Wendy said. "We don't have vanilla or cookies and cream?"

"The good folks at Total Fitness Corporation were nice enough to donate all the supplements to us. I didn't feel right being picky," Julius said. "Besides, ain't nothing wrong with chocolate, am I right?"

"It is because you are negro, yes?" Boris said.

"Boris, you giant retard, I'd kick your ass if you couldn't crush me," Julius said.

He popped open the tub and started ladling scoops into a large commercial blender. Adding peanut butter, coconut milk, and ice, Julius blended it until it was a smooth and creamy concoction. Using a soup ladle, he served up helpings in large glasses. He waited until everyone had a cup in front of them.

"Now that everyone has a glass, I wanted to welcome everyone to Camp Tum Tum. Today, we are all making history as we are the counselors of the first ever exclusive weight loss camp for the rich and powerful. You have all been chosen to be here, being the best in your field. Except for you college kids, your job is to shut up, listen, and do what is asked of you."

The kids nodded their heads that they understood. Julius smiled.

"This camp is something unlike anything ever seen before. We will slim down these brats and their wealthy parents will reward us greatly. We just need to stay the course and do our jobs well. We all know how to be professionals, but now we must act as them. Like I said before, no sex, no drugs, no alcohol. Do not molest the kids. Do not yell at the kids. You can encourage them, get a little tough on them, but don't hurl insults and make them want to quit. We can't have that."

"What if they no lift the weight I ask them to lift? I can hit them, yes? Just not hard? I not understand." Boris said.

"Boris, before you do anything, just ask me first. Give them weight they can lift and everything should be fine. Now everyone, raise a glass and pound this shit down. To Camp Tum Tum, and to changing the lives of these sad, fat kids."

"To Camp Tum Tum!" the room shouted, and all glasses emptied within seconds. A loud cheer went up and high-fives were exchanged.

Julius smiled as he wiped a protein shake mustache off his lips. He knew it was going to be an interesting summer.

***

"So the boss said no sex. I figured you'd want to get filled up before tomorrow begins," Collin said, staring down Wendy. Maxwell laughed.

"No, that's okay. I've found some company for tonight."

Wendy walked up to Boris and entwined her arms in his. The Russian smiled like he'd just won a weight lifting competition.

"You two can have fun tonight," Wendy said. Maxwell and Collin glanced at one another and shook their heads in disgust.

"She means you can have the faggot sex," Boris said.

"Thanks, Boris," Collin said.

"Yeah, we got it big man." Maxwell sighed.

"Want to try to bone one of the interns? We can Eiffel Tower like we did back in the old days?" Collin said, staring at the cluster of students talking amongst themselves.

"Sadly, I'm going to have to sit this one out. My stomach doesn't feel right. Too much protein, I think. Might need to fire off a deuce and get some of this out my system."

"Definitely too much info, bro. Have a good night." Collin patted Maxwell on the back as he lumbered off to his room.

Now that Maxwell had mentioned it, Collin didn't feel so hot either. Sweat formed on his brow and his mouth was dry. He hoped there wasn't a virus going around. He'd feel like one of those fat losers working out if he had to lead class sick. He decided the smart thing would be to turn in.

He bid everyone a good night and went to his bedroom. The moment he saw the toilet, the urge to vomit overcame him and he fell to the floor, puking into the porcelain throne. He dry heaved for another few minutes until the feeling subsided. Crawling into bed, he felt a chill rush down his spine and his body ached. *Fuck, I'm really sick.* He pulled the covers up high, figuring his world class body and healthy immune system would knock this virus out overnight. He closed his eyes, and never opened them again.

***

Olga and Melton entered Julius' sleeping chambers. It was 10 AM and no counselors had emerged to serve breakfast or lead class. The campers thought this was some kind of test of their willpower. They'd failed miserably as most had started raiding the kitchen after an hour. Olga and Melton, being two of the older campers, offered to check on the situation. As they entered the dark room, they thought this wasn't such a great idea anymore.

"Mr. Julius," Olga said, lightly tapping the door. "Sir, are you awake?"

"None of the counselors are around and we are hungry," Melton said.

"Melton, shut up. Mr. Julius, are you awake?"

"Are you sure he's even here? I bet they're just fucking with us."

The pair entered the suite and stood in the small living room. They looked around, and seeing nothing out of place, proceeded to the bedroom. Julius was in bed, his back to the door.

"Jeez, they get on us about being lazy," Melton said. "Julius, wake up. My parents aren't paying you to sleep all day." Melton pushed on the camp leader's back and immediately retracted his hand.

"What?"

"His . . . his skin. It's cold and gross feeling."

The momentum of Melton's push caused Julius' body to roll forward. His mouth was covered in white foam and his glazed-over eyes stared at the two campers.

"Oh my God, he's—"

"Dead!" Olga screamed and ran out of the suite. Melton quickly followed.

CHAPTER SEVEN

From the Diary of Jenny Running Bear, Camp Tum Tum Day Three:

Dear Diary,

I've finally found the time to write. It has been horrible but I must stay strong. Hopefully, I will be reading this again some day, thanking the universe for allowing me to make it through. If someone else is reading this, pray for us. So, for the sake of posterity:

My name is Jennifer Running Bear. Jenny is preferred. My parents are Lloyd and Eileen Running Bear. They co-own the Falling River Casino in Mt. Pleasant, Michigan. I have a weight problem and had been recruited to Camp Tum Tum after an incident. I may go into it later. I may not. I am a 4.0 student going into my last year of high school and I am planning on going to college and getting an English degree. My parents think I'm possessed by the 'white devil.' They don't understand anything. The real power, the real change . . . the real savior of our people is not wrapped up in fleecing seventy-year-old crackers out of their social security checks. Every time one of them puts a dollar into the Chief Double Down slot machine my Dad smiles. He's happy about the dollar and equates power to money. But our people still live in squalor on a Reservation. They take the money they are owed from the casino and buy McDonalds and booze and PlayStations. We are them. The real power will come from words. Powerful words. Journalistic words.

Like I said, no one understands me. The other fourteen volumes of diary entries will attest to the fact that I've beaten that horse to death . . . but you deserved to know who I really am. I don't feel very powerful right now. In fact, I feel scared and small and weak. And hungry. I say no one understands me quite a bit, but it's true. No one likes me, either. I volunteer, I help the homeless, I'm a good student and I try to fit in but it never seems to work. Never eat alone; there is no one to tell you that you should stop. We're not alone here, either. All of the campers are here and all right. There are twenty five of us, I believe. I'm still learning names. A boy named Charles has directed a bit of the traffic since . . . the event. Another boy, Miles, is helping him. I'm not sold on Charles, but the other one is very nice. And helpful. He was the only one willing to help.

The camp itself is complete chaos. I had been recruited by Julius, I think most of us here were, and we had all been prepared for a difficult few weeks but nothing could prepare us for what Day Two brought. I'm still trying to piece what happened together, and have been working non-stop nearly twenty-four hours. I will try and convey what happened chronologically, at least as much as I know.

All of the staffers at Camp Tum Tum are fitness experts and dieticians. The counselors double as the cooking staff and the administration. That was done, as it was explained to me, in order to reduce communication breakdowns and so that the staff had a 'whole body' approach to the campers. They knew exactly what we're taking into our bodies, since they were cooking it, and knew our limits in physical activity. There was a staff to camper, 1 to 2 ratio when we arrived two days ago. I liked that. It showed that we would be held accountable to someone personally. They are all dead now, of course.

One of the bigger girls (and I do not mean older) Olga and another boy were the first ones to see what had happened. The campers had gathered, ready to go, for the morning activities but no staffers had appeared as of yet. They went to Julius' cabin and, well, they came back out of breath and terrified.

I had mentioned that, while working at my parents' casino, I had trained with the on-site EMTs and knew some basic medical things. It's just something to say, you know? New people, they want to know interesting things. All eyes turned to me and I volunteered to check it out. All we could get from Olga and the other kid was "Julius" and "not hungry anymore" between gasps. As I headed out the door, the rest of the campers just watched me go. Except for Miles. He asked if he could go with me and I thought that was sweet. Well, he didn't so much ask but he mumbled something and sweated a lot. I took that as a formal request.

We exited the common area building and turned left. The staff cabins are about fifteen feet from the common building to the south and the camper cabins are about fifteen feet from the common building to the north. Miles and I made it to Julius' front door and pushed inside. From what we gathered, we wouldn't be interrupting him at all.

The smell hit me first and then Miles. We both gagged. I don't know if anyone reading this has dealt with a dead body before, but I have. About once a year one of the blue-haired future millionaires that my parents call customers would die on the gaming floor. Stroke, heart attack, seizure, just being really old . . . you name it and they've probably died from it at the Falling River. It's no wonder, though. I've actually seen a man with a stoma, a hole in his neck to breathe, smoking a cigarette through his neck hole. It's amazing what people will do to themselves. Absolutely amazing. What people don't think about when someone dies, especially when it is sudden and unexpected is that their bowels release. Everywhere.

But, back to Julius. We gagged when we entered the room and I knew that something really bad had happened. We entered the bedroom and Julius was seated, eyes wide and staring. He was dead, of course. I can only assume it was some kind of food poisoning. None of the campers are affected and our immune systems are in far worse shapes than the staffers so it isn't a powerful airborne bacterium. The first clue was the froth and vomit caked around Julius' lips. It had run down his chest and dried there like a peach-colored Santa beard. His eyes were red with every blood vessel broken so I knew that he had been vomiting. He was in boxer shorts and seated on the ground in a massive puddle of feces. If it weren't for the boxers, we wouldn't have known where Julius stopped and the puddle began. From what I could tell, this was far more than a simple contraction and release at the moment of death. There was a trail of fecal matter from the bathroom area into the bedroom. It would appear that Julius was trying to make it somewhere and failed. Either there was too much pain or he was too weak.

I hadn't noticed that Miles was missing until I turned around to ask him a question. I found him outside, running for the next staffer's cabin. He opened the door and, before he could even get inside, he retched as the smell of another dead fitness expert wafted out on an island breeze. It was like that, over and over again. Miles and I rushed back to the common building and told the others. Panic is an understatement. I understand that we are all here for a common reason, but I didn't expect things to dissolve so quickly.

When we reported that the staff was . . . dead, sorry, that is just hard to write, the kid that was with Olga and a few others stormed the kitchen. After a moment, thinking that they were missing out on something, the rest of the campers piled in after them. I could tell that Miles wanted to get in there and chew on something to relieve the stress, but it felt like he didn't want to leave me. I tried to tell them that what happened to the staffers had to be a food-related issue, but they didn't pay attention. Except for Miles and Charles. Miles, I could tell, was using every ounce of strength he had not to bury his face in a pile of oyster crackers. Charles was different. He looked at the campers feasting, eating everything in sight, and he smiled. When I saw that I got a funny feeling in the pit of my stomach. I think, right then, things just got worse but I couldn't place my finger on it.

I'm an emotional eater. When things get stressful, I eat. That is why most of us are here at Tum Tum.

Dead camp staff is incredibly stressful, apparently, and it didn't take long for the twenty-two campers that raided the kitchen to virtually wipe out twelve weeks worth of meals. Logic and rational thought took a back seat to a feeding frenzy that would put Ancient Rome to shame. This was Caligula-level here. That is when Charles stepped up.

Charles reminded us that the other twenty-two had just consumed virtually all of our food. There was one satellite phone on the island for emergencies and Julius had it locked in his room. The phone box was only accessible to staff and they each had to memorize a seven digit code that would unlock the keypad. Apparently, we were stuck. Charles said that he had a plan, though, and he would see us through the other side and all would be well.

I'm not sure I believed him then or now. The other campers blinked their way out of a food coma and finally paid attention to the gravity of the situation. Charles stood over them and opened his arms and, I swear to you, they came to him. Each one of those gluttonous fools came to Charles and hugged him or patted him on the back. They thanked him and told him that they had complete confidence in his abilities.

I wasn't sure what I was really seeing. I realize that I may be a bit more literate than the rest of the gang here. I also know that kids with problems like mine are usually very susceptible to influence. This was some crazy Jonestown stuff, though. Miles looked to me and I could only nod. For the time being, it would be in our best interest to go with the flow. I mean, we have to be here, we have to wait for someone to realize things aren't quite right over at Camp Tum Tum. Charles, though . . .

I didn't disagree with his first 'request,' though. He's a smart guy and we both realized that so many corpses, in a tropical climate, can be a huge health risk. So, with the help of a few others, we spent the remainder of the afternoon getting the staffers piled up and ready for a bonfire. It was sad, and there were many tears. It took a while since most of us had to take breaks every few minutes, but we managed to get it done. Charles will light it up this evening.

As we collected the staffers, though, I thought that someone should keep a record of what we found so, after all this is over, there can be some closure for their families. I gathered all of the information I could. It is folded and in the back of this diary.

If you're reading this and you're not me, I'm sorry.

Need sleep.

JRB

***

Camp Tum Tum Staff

I'm so sorry. —JRB

Julius Washington—Julius was found as I described in my diary. There was some sort of food illness, I think. His eyes were bloodshot and protruding from his head like he had been vomiting profusely. A great deal of fecal matter led from the bathroom to where he was found, a trail of about six feet. It looked like the last few feet he may have been dragging his legs. From what he told us, Julius was like me and the others at one point. He worked hard to get where he was at now and even though I didn't know him long, I will miss him.

Collin Lamb—Aqua Aerobics. Collin died in his bathroom. He appeared to be in worse shape than

Julius. One of Collin's eyes apparently burst or was ruptured when his head slammed down onto the toilet seat in the lavatory. The bowl was filled with a dark-brown vomit and it looks as if he did not have the strength to reach up and flush it down before he passed on. The tell-tale pool of feces, with the same liquid consistency and volume, spread out underneath Collin. I hadn't met him yet but I've saved his wallet in a bag with the others.

Boris Nakitoff—Strength and Conditioning & Wendy Latrine—Aerobics. Boris and Wendy were found together. They were both naked and on the living room floor of Wendy's cabin. I can only guess what they were up to when the effects of whatever this is hit them. From what I can piece together, I believe that Wendy was the first casualty here. From the amount of vomit crusted around Boris' pelvic area, the onset came as a shock. She was a petite woman so food poisoning would be quick and brutal. Her eyes were bloodshot but it appears that she did not suffer long. Boris, on the other hand, does not appear to be affected by the food poisoning. More accurately, he died before it could hit him. It is evident that Boris slipped and fell backwards, probably after Wendy's problems started to spray themselves all over, like when you put your thumb over the garden hose. The bottom of Boris' feet are caked in fecal matter that could only have come from Wendy so that can paint a picture of how his head connected with the corner of a coffee table. There is a large wound and pieces of bone scattered underneath his head. I had met them briefly and, aside from the bodily fluids, they look as if they would make a cute couple.

Maxwell Powers—Cardio Coach. Max was the last

one we found. Like the others, his eyes were distended, vomit and fecal matter spread throughout the room. Getting Maxwell taken care of was a bit more difficult. He was kneeling on a chair and had a jump rope tied around his neck. The jump rope was then looped around a coat hook on the bedroom door. I'd seen this in movies but, wow. Rigor had set in, obviously, and we had a tremendous time prying Maxwell's fingers off of his own penis and getting him out to the bonfire area. He seemed like a nice man.

The Interns—We are still looking for identification for the six college kids that were interning on Camp Tum Tum. They were introduced to us, briefly, at dinner the night before, but I think everyone was too hungry to notice. The interns shared a cabin and were all found together. Same symptoms, same cause of death. I don't think I can write anymore.

CHAPTER EIGHT

Letter Home, Day Eleven: Landish, Miles

Hello mother, hello father,

I don't know why I'm writing this, maybe to clear it all in my head, you know? Maybe when we're rescued I can use these letters to piece together what happened. I read about post traumatic stress disorder. If I could forget this place, I would. Firstly, I should apologize. I know that you were only thinking of me and my health when you shipped me off to Camp Tum Tum and I understand that I wasn't the kind of son you had hoped for. I get that now. I also understand why I need to be here, at this moment. The things we've had to do have been horrible. That's for sure! But I think I needed this to realize how much potential I have and that I am able to tap into. Our situation isn't the best on the island, but I've finally found someplace where I can make a difference!

We burned the bodies of the camp staff today. Jenny says it was either a food borne illness, like food poisoning, or some strange stomach virus. She is probably the smartest person on the island, which is saying a lot, and she said we needed to eliminate any potential health risks. That's a quote. I told you she was smart. Charles agreed with her so we got to work. The smell was awful, sort of. We had been getting hungrier and hungrier after the kitchen incident. Oh, I should tell you about that.

When the campers figured out that the staffers were dead and we didn't have any way of communicating with the mainland, things went a little crazy. Everyone, except for me, Jenny and Charles, completely raided the kitchen. Everyone shoved whatever they could in their mouths. This one kid, Melton? He found Jules first and was pretty messed up about it. When he ran out of food he started choking down baking flour. It was pretty gruesome. Jenny called it a mass psychosis but it was way worse. It was like that story from *Jaws* where all of the guys left after a battleship sunk and were in life-preservers, just floating around when a big school of sharks just up and ate most of them. The stuff in the coolers, all of the canned food . . . all of it gone. There was no red meat or pork on the island, on purpose, and nothing full of sugar so at least they all loaded up on carbs and starches and not fat, but wow. Someone, I forget who, realized that all the food was gone. After that, the panic set in until Charles stepped up.

I'm pretty lucky to be friends with him. I don't know where we'd be without him here right now. Charles got everyone calmed down. It was real cool to see and everyone knew that he was my roommate so that was pretty cool, too. When they all panicked he stood there and was confident that he could find food and sustain us for however long it took for help to arrive. I mean, it was like he was born for this. Kids like Melton and this black kid Albert were completely off in outer space, crying and wailing and losing it.

Charles walked up to each one of them, whispered in their ear and they calmed down. Just like that. I couldn't believe it.

Jenny leaned over to me and called him the lard whisperer but I didn't laugh (even though I thought it was kind of funny). Jenny isn't so big on Charles, she doesn't trust him. I bet she's like that all the time, though. I'll work on her. I really want her and Charles to get along. He asked me to help him take care of some things so that makes me second in charge, I guess. Would you have ever believed that? I'm in charge of something! So, I'll work on Jenny. I think she's really a cool girl. This may come as a shock to you, but I think she might like me, too.

Charles got the campers situated. He asked Jenny to be in charge of the medical stuff and she agreed. Even she could see how much sense that made and he asked this blonde girl, Freda Packer, to take charge of the female campers. He is really organized. His first idea was to organize ourselves to explore the island. Coming in we could see that there was a ton of jungle out there, so foraging for bananas, citrus fruits, coconuts . . . all of that would be good. Charles also took a quick survey of who has had some hunting experience or camping experience. As you can imagine, not many of us have. Regardless, Charles is going to lead a bunch of us out in the morning to hunt for game. We've got some javelins and bows and arrows from the fitness compound and it can't be too difficult, right?

I know I'm talking about Charles a lot, but it just blows me away. Here is a kid that looks like me and has the same amount of friends back home that I do (zero) and plays video games and everything. He just took control of the situation. I like to think that I would do the same thing, but I don't know. I feel good that he's taking charge. I know that the other kids do, too. Melton and Albert especially. It's almost creepy the way they look at Charles now, but they were in a bad spot.

I'll continue to work on Jenny, she'll see what's going on before too long. Hopefully, we'll all get through this and I can introduce you guys to her. She rocks.

I know I didn't say it a lot, but I love you both. I hope we get to read these together.

Love,
Miles

CHAPTER NINE

MILES HAD THE deer in his sights and pulled back on the string. Holding his breath, he let the arrow fly. It hit the tree with a loud *thunk*, and the deer sprinted into the brush, invisible in seconds. He sighed and cursed under his breath. Video games had not prepared him for this.

"Did you get him?" Charles came running up behind him, breathing heavily. He stopped inches behind Miles, wheezing and sputtering.

"Missed," Miles said, defeated.

"Goddammit, Miles. What, exactly, are you good for? I thought you said you could do this?"

"I thought I could. This isn't like the games I play. I figured it would be as easy as point and shoot."

Disgusted, Charles left Miles' side and turned to address the jiggling mass of sweaty, flabby figures behind him. Miles joined them, and let his bow hit the ground. Wiping his damp forehead, he tried not to gag as the aroma of the other hunters engulfed him. Foul, rancid onion-like vapors seemed to choke the air, and Miles was starting to regret getting so close to this motley crew of wannabe hunters. There were five others, not including him or Charles, and the boys held either a bow from the archery closet or a javelin which served as a spear.

"Men, this isn't going very well. We need to find food, and quick. If I'd realized sooner that all the other fat asses had eaten our entire inventory, I'd have put a stop to it."

"You were eating right along with the rest of us," Tommy Wheeler said.

"What did you say to me?" Charles' face darkened.

"You heard me. You ate as much as anyone, if not more. Stop putting the blame on everyone else."

A thick fist flew through the air and Tommy collapsed to the ground, gripping his bloody nose. Charles stood over him, ready to continue the assault. He relented.

"Ingrate. I stopped you before you ate each other! If you want another one of those, Tommy, just speak out of line again. I can do much worse than that."

Tommy stumbled to his feet and wiped the blood on his sleeve. Miles could see tears well in the boy's eyes, but Tommy did his best to fight them from coming down. Miles had no clue what Charles would have done had the boy started to cry in front of him. He wanted to get up and push Charles down. Make the chubby dictator feel powerless, but he was too afraid. Charles had the other hunters trained like robots, and Miles feared they would turn on him, instead of helping in the coup. *Someone is going to get really hurt because of that . . . his got serious, fast.*

"Since that's out of the way, let's resume hunting. We need to come back with something." Charles surveyed the area, as if looking for something to kill.

"There're all kinds of plants. Maybe we can find something to eat?" one of the boys suggested.

"I'm not grazing on some grass like a fucking cow!" Charles kicked a clump of sticks into the brush. "We are going to come back with meat. We are hunters and we are men. We will provide for the others."

The rest of the hunting party stayed silent, not wanting to make eye contact with their volatile leader.

"We will split up into groups and cover more ground. Miles and Tommy, you are with me. The rest, stick together, and you better come back with something."

Miles sighed. He wasn't sure why Charles singled him out and he was unsure why Tommy was coming with them. Tommy was a nice kid, but the guy was a clumsy oaf who couldn't walk or breathe quietly to save his life. Killing something to eat, let alone finding it, was going to be difficult.

The groups parted and trudged off into different directions. Miles located a worn-down path and the three traversed it, their eyes scanning the thick woods for any kind of movement. Charles led the way, with Miles close behind. Tommy straggled back a few yards, and Miles could still hear him crashing through bushes, doing all he could to make noise. Charles shot him ugly looks every few moments, but kept quiet.

"I'm really thinking of cutting Tommy loose," Charles said.

"What do you mean?" Miles was confused.

"I mean look at him. Fat, clumsy, and stupid. The trifecta of worthlessness."

"I don't think fat should be a factor. After all, every person on this island fits that category."

"Yeah, but there are fat kids like you and me who can actually do stuff without being a complete mess, and then there are people like him. The dead weight. The takers. He'll never help us survive, only slow us down, and worse, he'll take food out of our mouths."

"Jesus, Charles. Tommy might be a bit clumsy, but what are you saying? Let the guy starve? We can't do that. Besides, we might get rescued any day now. Someone will notice when no one reports in from the camp."

"It's been a while now, and we still haven't seen anyone. We can make this place work, but I need people like you who can help with the situation, not slow it down." Charles glanced back at Tommy and shook his head in disgust.

"We're just hungry. Once we eat, we'll have a clearer head. I agree with you that we need to do a better job assigning tasks to people who can actually do them. I don't think Tommy makes for a good hunter."

As if on cue, Tommy slipped on a moss covered rock and hit the ground. He let out a squeal of pain as he held his knee. His javelin lay on the ground next to him. Miles ran to his side.

"You okay, Tommy?"

"My knee! I don't think I can walk. It's broken!"

"It's not broken you fat baby. Get the fuck up and keep your voice down." Charles joined them.

"I can't. I can't do this anymore." Tommy sobbed.

"Kid, you fell on your ass, not your knee. Stop crying and get up. Just get through today and you won't have to hunt anymore." Charles held his hand out.

Tommy eyed it suspiciously, but took it. Charles hoisted him to his feet.

"Now pick up your spear and let's move."

The three continued their trek with Tommy once again falling behind. His thick snorts and coughs echoed through the woods. Miles looked at Charles and saw him grow angrier with each passing sound.

A deer crossed their path, bending down to feast on tender grasses. Charles and Miles froze, smiling at one another. The animal was only feet away, a shot Miles knew even he could hit.

"Let's both draw and shoot," Charles whispered.

They raised their bows in unison, not making a sound and trying not to breathe. The deer was lined up, and soon two arrows would fly, cutting the majestic animal down to save the camp.

"On three we shoot," Miles said, his lips barely moving.

The deer continued to eat, oblivious of its impending demise.

"One . . . two . . . —" Miles said.

"Hey guys, look! A deer!" Tommy said, running up to them.

The deer shot off like a rocket. Miles let the arrow go, but it stuck the tree where the deer had stood. He couldn't believe it. They had dinner, and now it was gone. He seethed with anger and wanted to hit Tommy. If Charles was going to do something, Miles knew he wouldn't stop him.

"Oh, man. You guys missed?" Tommy said.

"Nope," Charles replied, and shot his arrow into Tommy's stomach.

The boy screamed and hit the ground. Blood gushed from his gut, and his hands gripped the bolt. A look of panic, fear, and confusion was plastered on his pale face. Miles stood dumbfounded.

"Charles, no! What have you done?" Miles said.

"Doing what I said. I'm cutting down the dead weight. You fucked up for the last time Tommy-boy, you fat worthless shit head." Charles picked up the javelin and descended on the mortally wounded boy.

All Miles could do was watch as Charles lifted the javelin and jabbed it into Tommy again and again. After five stabs, Tommy stopped screaming, and the forest was silent again. A lonely bird chirped from a tree, and Miles felt the world rush on him in one violent surge. He fell to his knees and vomited into the grass. His stomach was empty, and strings of phlegm and bile sluiced onto the ground.

"There. That takes care of that problem." Charles stabbed the javelin into the dirt next to Tommy's head.

Miles saw the look of terror and anguish frozen on the dead boy's face. He felt another wave of nausea crash into him.

"Come on, Miles. Stop being so dramatic and get up," Charles said. He pulled Miles to his feet.

"How could you do that? Why would you do that?"

"He fucked us out of dinner tonight. That deer was dead to rights, and he blew it not only for you and me, but the entire camp. If we are going to make this work, then we need to rid the population of the ones who will bring us down. It had to be done."

"What are you going to tell everyone?"

"Well I'm not going to lie. They will understand, and if they don't," Charles picked the javelin up and rotated in the air, "I'll make them understand."

"What are we going to do with his . . . body?"

"Drag it back to camp. We aren't savages, Miles. I'm not going to leave it out here for the animals to eat. I'll find the others and bring them back. You stay here so we don't lose it." Charles trudged down the path, whistling a happy tune to himself.

Miles stared at Tommy, who glared back at him with lifeless eyes. A shiver went down his spine, and he knew something evil had just entered Camp Tum Tum.

CHAPTER TEN

From the Official Record of the Reign of Charles York, Prime Minister of Tum Tum Island

Things are falling into place. I can just feel it. The campers, my subjects, are respecting me more and more with each passing day, and they should. I'm one motherfucker who demands respect.

I'm giving them the one thing they've wanted but could never achieve: paradise. But instead they want to wallow around all day; just like the fat hogs they've been called all their lives. Well not me. I have a plan, and I'll see it to fruition.

My parents were smart—or were they lucky?—to send me here when they did. In doing so, they saved their lives. I planned on killing them that night, but was intercepted at my school and sent to this terrible place without even seeing them. It's almost like they knew, and though I knew about this place, I thought I had more time.

I dream about their death, what I had planned, and smile. You know how people say money can't buy happiness? Well, they are wrong. Most who say that have never had money to begin with, so their opinion holds absolutely no value. I'm not talking about having an extra thousand dollars in the bank account. That isn't money. That's nothing. I'm talking real money. So much that it allows you to do whatever you want. It can buy your freedom. It can buy secrets. And it can buy the finest grade of poison that cannot be traced to anyone. I need control! I need to lead! I was born to do this, and it wasn't happening in New York.

Even when you are the richest kid in school, you can't buy respect. That's really the only thing money can't get you. You can surround yourself with a bunch of ass-kissers and yes-men, but that isn't the same. People have to fear you, and that must be earned. I have what I want now. I have respect. Sure, someone had to die for me to get it, but I'd slaughter every person here to just have one of them bow to me. With the meat-head counselors gone, these poor misguided fatties need someone to guide them. I rule this place.

Did you know my anger problem was blamed on my weight? It had to be that. It could never have been the years of physical, emotional, and mental abuse. No! That's just absurd. Surely the hottest girl in school asking me to homecoming and then laughing in my face when I said yes had nothing to do with why I hate the world. The kids calling me a fat ass for just eating lunch didn't jade me in any way. Nope. It's all the weight's fault, the doctor said. What a quack! The decision was made to ship me off to fat camp, and though Tum Tum knew they were getting another camper, they didn't know they'd be getting me.

It's becoming clearer why I killed Tommy Wheeler, son of the rock legend Ricky Wheeler. Just before I was shipped here, this prick named Peter Manning picked the wrong time to fuck with me. I was in class, just quietly doing the assignment, not bothering anyone. Then the poking started. And the pig grunts. And the laughing! It was when he pushed the back of my head that I lost it, and my pen ended up in his eye. His screams were almost comical. My parents are still dealing with that lawsuit. Amazing how I avoided jail, but was still sentenced to a prison term.

When I stabbed Tommy with the javelin, all I could see was Peter's stupid, smiling face. His screams sounded like pig squeals, and I must admit I did black out a bit during the kill. It was a true *out-of-body* experience and I watched myself do it. And, I must admit, I looked so damn cool. Perfect form if I must say. Poor Miles. I'm still cracking up over the look on his face. But he'll be all right, and I know he'll fall in line. He just doesn't have what it takes to lead, which is a shame because it'd have been nice to have him as a second in command. He is popular and an asset, but I don't need him. In truth, I don't need any of them.

Tommy's death will not have been in vain. He'll help us survive in more ways than he could ever have known. His ultimate sacrifice will power us through this rough patch while I try to sort out our food situation. Luckily, the fatties didn't touch a small selection of the raw vegetables during their eating binge. I just need to use something to stretch out what we have. Maybe a soup? I don't know yet.

There are a few campers here who do show some potential to serve under me. I have a few selected as personal guards and enforcers. After all, I can't be everywhere at once. Jenny Running Bear, while having a stupid name, is going to work out great as our medic. Freda Packer will be in charge of our food inventory once we get a better handle on it. She'll also take care of me in other ways. After all, a king needs someone to help relieve his stress. She's already hinted to being down for it, and I'm in no position to say no. I'll present them to the campers tonight. A good meal should get everyone's spirits high, but heaven help any who oppose my plans.

Everyone will fall in line. I just know it. Honestly, they'll have no choice, but it's not like going back home is any better for them. We have everything we need here. Water, shelter, medicine, and we'll be fine with food. I know we will. This island is huge and we'll explore it thoroughly. I just have to mold them into willing servants. It's our only chance of survival. If some must die so the society can flourish, well, so be it.

I have to go, but I'll write more later as the ideas come. For now, I have to decide what to do about Tommy's body and how to best honor him for this evening.

***

Chicken Soup for the Soul Surprise, a recipe from the kitchen of Freda Packer

Original recipe makes 100 servings

30 pounds Whole Chicken Surprise (surprise . . . it isn't chicken)
40 carrots, halved
40 stalks celery, halved
10 large onion, halved
Water to cover
Salt and pepper to taste

Directions

Place the "chicken," carrots, celery and onion in a pot that can hold all of it and cover with cold water. It has to be cold; we want things to cook together. Heat and simmer, with no lid, until the "chicken" meat falls off of the bones (skim off foam when necessary). The foam can be tricky. It will be greasy. This may sound strange, but I recommend a spatula. I know, there are holes in a spatula, but trust me on this one.

After simmering, and testing the meat to make sure it is cooked through, take it all out of the pot and strain the liquid. That will be your broth. Pick the "chicken" off the bones (it should be falling right off at that point) and finely chop the vegetables when vegetables are available. Season to taste. When finished, simply return it all to the pot, stir, and serve.

CHAPTER ELEVEN

A FEW DAYS HAD passed since the debacle labeled 'The Big Hunt,' and Charles plotted his next move with precision before he assembled the campers together in the dining area. Complaints of hunger and fatigue persisted, and Charles did his best to compose himself, though on the inside he wanted to lash out at the whiny group of fatties. The returning hunters had broken the lack of success to the group and spirits were low. A gloom settled in the room, infecting each camper and oozing over the area like one of the campers over a folding chair.

Miles shuffled into the room with Jenny at his side. He kept the story of Charles killing Tommy to himself, and still couldn't believe what he'd witnessed. In the following days, he'd tried to come up with some reason to justify Charles' actions, but just couldn't. What Charles had done was savage and brutal. It was murder in its most carnal sense, and had they been in civilization, no amount of money would be able to buy Charles out of this jam.

Jenny noticed Miles' unusual silence, ever since he'd returned from the hunt, and chalked it up to low blood sugar and a lack of prowess as a hunter. She tried to tell him it wasn't like the video games he'd spent hours playing. Real hunting took skill, self-discipline, and inner strength. The group had been full of vigor and optimism before they'd left. It was amazing what half a mile of walking through underbrush did to the group's spirits. She tried one last time before they sat down in the dining hall and awaited Charles' arrival. He was another issue altogether, but Miles came first. She'd felt a spark and thought perhaps Miles felt the same way.

"Look, we'll manage. I'm sure with a little more foraging we'll be able to survive! My people were hunters and gatherers. If there is one thing I know it's how to collect the fruit of the land."

"Sure." Miles slumped into the nearest chair and stared at his feet.

Jenny sighed. She was about to give it one more, valiant, effort, when Charles strolled into the room. She was surprised to see his procession enter the room first.

Flanked by Melton on one side and another older kid who looked solidly muscled, underneath the flab, named Clarence Rutherford, Jenny believed, Charles strode into the room. The grumbling group of campers hushed and all eyes turned to the beaming dictator. Melton raised his voice.

"All hail Prime Minister Charles York of Camp Tum Tum!"

Charles stepped forward, smiling. He waved to the assembled group. A few campers clapped, but the majority just stared in disbelief.

"Prime Minister," Jenny declared under her breath. Miles nodded his head. "You knew about this? For how long?"

Miles didn't have a chance to answer as Charles'

voice rang out across the dining hall.

"Friends," he began, "I know that this may seem presumptuous, but I assure you, and Camp Tum Tum, are in good hands. I don't want you to feel as if this is some sort of power play or a vain attempt in making me feel more important than I truly am. I care about you. We are in this together and, after your show of support during the Kitchen Incident of our first day together, I felt compelled to formally take the mantle here and become responsible for all of us."

The scattered clapping increased in intensity this time. Jenny could only stare ahead, her mouth agape. *Charles York? Prime Minister?* It still hadn't registered.

"Furthermore," Charles continued, "I feel compelled to introduce my cabinet to you. These fine individuals have decided, like me, that they desired to provide a civil, safe existence here for us all. You've met them already, but allow me to introduce these fine individuals to you once again in their new roles. Melton and Clarence, my faithful friends, who have graciously agreed to help me facilitate a new beginning for us here, will serve as my Chief of Staff and Secretary of Defense, respectively."

Jenny looked around the room. Every face stared upward, pie-eyed and smiling. *They are actually believing this . . . this . . . bullshit!* She turned to Miles whose eyes remained at his feet. "Miles, please tell me you didn't know about this."

He shrugged. Jenny looked around the room again, transfixed by the bizarre scene.

"Miles Landish, join me up here," Charles called out.

Miles looked up. He glanced at Jenny, making only the most perfunctory eye contact, and stood.

"Miles?" she asked.

"Sorry." He muttered the word, his head hanging low. Miles shuffled over to Charles who awaited him with arms open wide. The Prime Minister embraced Miles and spun him to face the assembled campers.

"Ladies and gentlemen, may I present to you my Vice Minister!"

The spattering of applause grew with each successive moment. The campers appeared to be accepting this new regime. They were lost, hungry, and afraid. Thousands of miles away from their mansions and comfort foods, they needed someone to take charge. Charles York rose to the challenge.

Jenny saw the displeasure on Miles' face. She could only guess what kind of awfulness had occurred to make Miles choose to be in Charles' cabinet. She understood the teen Prime Minister was charismatic, but she'd never really trusted him and thought Miles felt the same way. It was all too much. This mockery of political machinations had to be brought to a screeching halt. Jenny addressed the self-crowned king.

"Prime Minister!"

Miles' eyes went wide in panic. He motioned toward Jenny in subtle waves, trying desperately to get her to sit down. He'd witnessed Charles angry, and the results were something from a horror movie. Charles stepped forward and addressed Jenny.

"Yes, Jenny."

"You want to lead *us*? What about that failed hunting party you led?"

The assembled campers shook off the euphoria of false hope. That hollow, empty feeling crept back in. The campers turned back to Charles, the smattering of applause replaced with grumbling of both voice and stomach. A few campers stood and appeared to want to leave, but sat back down unsure of what they would do next. Jenny thought they resembled cows in a field with an open gate.

Sensing the tension building, Clarence and Melton moved toward the campers. The heat in the room seemed to rise as tempers flared.

Charles pushed through his honor guard and stared Jenny down.

"I understand your pain and, believe me, your hunger! But, trust me, the hunting party wasn't a total waste of time." Charles made sure his voice could be heard over the sounds of unrest. He glared at Jenny. She smirked back, challenging him and what she considered a puppet regime. To her surprise, Charles returned the smile and Jenny knew something awful was about to happen. Jenny glanced over to Miles who shook his head vigorously. What had she just done?

"Everyone here has heard the hunting trip was a failure, when in fact we didn't come home empty handed. So, let me introduce to you my Prime Mistress, and Secretary of Rationing, Freda Packer."

The doors to the kitchen swung outward and a wonderful smell exploded from the entryway. Those sitting closest were first to fall silent to the smell they'd just experienced. The campers quieted as the beautiful aroma floated past them. The silence spread to where Charles and his cabinet stood proudly. Charles inhaled deeply, acknowledging the glorious scent that had wafted from the kitchen and pacified the unruly mob.

"Marginally successful means successful. My friends, let us feast!"

Freda rolled a large serving cart from the darkened kitchen into the light of the dining hall. A huge platter sat atop, piled high with a shredded meat. It was tender and juicy looking and the more discerning pallets could detect hints of basil, garlic, onion powder and thyme in the air. It smelled and looked like pulled pork.

Miles knew what was on that platter, but found himself transfixed by the sights and smells. It was divine. His stomach rumbled.

Jenny's mouth filled with saliva at the sight of the feast. She couldn't remember the last time she'd eaten and the prospect of food mesmerized her. She shook her head, trying to fight off the effects of a deep hunger. Miles had told her the hunting party had failed miserably. Charles wouldn't hunt on his own. The pile of meat didn't have a logical explanation. A sickly feeling crept into the back of her mind, forcing out the irrational thoughts caused by hunger. Fearing the worst, she backed toward the exit.

Charles smiled and turned to his subjects. He raised his arms in the air.

"Feast! Feast!" His voice rang through the hall.

The campers descended upon the meat like a pack of wild dogs. Miles resisted the urge to join them, but the heavenly smell pulled him to the pile of meat like a magnet. He turned away. Charles noticed and pulled his Vice Minister around, pointing him at the platter of slow-cooked, perfectly seasoned Tommy Wheeler.

"I can't," Miles said. He was unable to pull his eyes from the food.

"It was Tommy or us, you have to realize that." Charles whispered into his ear and a chill ran down Miles' back.

A moment of clarity washed over Miles as the hunger took hold, and he nodded in agreement with his master. Charles shoved him gently and Miles dove into the feast, joining his fellow campers.

A cry of horror escaped Jenny as Miles planted his face into a steaming pile of human flesh. She turned away from the gorging group of obese young people and did her best not to begin dry heaving.

Charles pulled Clarence and Melton away from the food.

"I need you to take care of Running Bear, do you understand?"

They nodded, glaring in Jenny's direction. She was no longer there. The door swung loosely on its frame, evidence of its recent use. They looked to their Prime Minister for guidance.

"Bring her to me," Charles said. Clarence and Melton headed out and Charles turned back to the feasting campers.

He held his hand out to Freda and she moved to him quickly. Charles took a moment to admire her large breasts lying over an ample stomach and curly, auburn hair that cascaded around her cherubic face. Freda met Charles in a violent, tongue-laden kiss. Their hands explored each other, and the standard-issue Camp Tum Tum t-shirts fell to the floor in a crumpled heap. They stared at one another, Charles shirtless, and Freda in a nude colored bra. Their heavy breathing resulted in both sets of breasts jiggling in unison.

The unexpected carnal moment captured the attention of a few of the campers. They looked up from their feasting and Charles turned to them. He reached his hand into the pile of pulled Tommy and held it over his head.

"I have something to tell you all that may be difficult to understand. As you have heard, the hunting trip was a bit of a failure, though not a complete one. The feast you are eating was not provided from the bosom of the forest that surrounds us."

The campers froze and, using a great deal of will power, turned their faces away from the diminishing pile of sustenance. Their grease-smeared cheeks glistened from the well-marbled meat. Charles, with the help of Freda, stepped up on a cafeteria chair that nearly buckled under his weight.

"You've been eating Tommy Wheeler, an unfortunate casualty of our hunting expedition. Friends, circumstances being what they are, it appears we'll have to consume human flesh to survive. This is a simple fact of our current situation and is a grim reality until a sustainable food source can be maintained."

Charles scanned the room. The realization of what they'd just heard dawned on the campers slowly. A few retched, sticking sausage-thick fingers down their throats in a futile attempt to vomit up the human meat. Others stared down at their hands, frozen in disbelief. Charles was pleasantly surprised when no one puked.

"Tommy Wheeler made the ultimate sacrifice and his death was not in vain. His death has sustained us. His death has made it possible for us to continue as a society. He's a true patriot and will be remembered fondly in years to come."

Miles looked at Charles, eyes welling with tears. He understood what was being said, and even rationalized the path they'd chosen, but he just couldn't believe he'd dined on another human. A person he'd known, albeit not for long, but still someone he'd spoken with and had a name, a family, and a life. The act was horrible, one of the vilest things a human could do, but the hunger was strong. He couldn't fight it any longer.

Finally, one of the campers rose and held her hands upward, as if in praise. Her lips smacked together as she spoke and a small piece of Tommy fell to the floor with a splat.

"Bless you, Charles!" She shoved a wad of Tommy into her greedy mouth, chewing and swallowing. She moaned in pleasure, as if the consumption of this flesh was orgasmic and went in for more.

The other campers followed her lead. Cries of "Bless you, Charles," and "Thank you," barely recognizable through mouths stuffed with meat, resonated through the hall. Charles laughed, his hands still clutching the wad of Tommy held high.

"Campers! We are no longer constrained by what society has determined for us. We are no longer the brunt of a thin society's jokes. The great law that I have for you, the one mandate that should dictate how we live together and," he paused and turned to Freda, "how we love together should only be governed by one decree."

The campers stared as Charles, with a swipe of his pudgy hands, dropped his sweat pants to reveal his naked nether region. He lifted his belly, revealing a small, under-utilized penis. He shoved the wad of Tommy in his mouth and masticated loudly while wiping the greasy remains on and around his penis. He swallowed and announced, chewed bits of meat flying from his mouth "Do what thou wilt!"

Freda buried her face in Charles' underbelly area, licking the meat juices off Charles' rock-hard erection.

Miles and the other campers stood shocked at the display of chubby fornication. The repressed hormones and sexual curiosity surged to the surface. They had been denied the touch of another human being for years. The only pleasure they'd known came from themselves, when physics was kind, and this new decree by their Prime Minister meant they were no longer forced to be outside the realm of beauty, monsters looking in the window. This was their society, and what they determined to be proper conduct had absolutely no bearing on the rest of the world. At last, they were free.

Camper turned to camper, young man to young woman, or young man to young man, or young woman to young woman, preferences decided upon quickly. No one was left out.

Miles tried to resist the wanton display of lust, but felt an urge that rivaled hunger bubbling up inside of him. A young female turned to him, ripping off her Camp Tum Tum shirt to reveal large, bare breasts that drooped over her stomach. Her nipples pointed at Miles' belly button but, being the first he had ever seen, he found them irresistible. They met in a fierce kiss, smearing the grease of the meal across each other's face.

Charles stood tall on the chair as Freda slammed her face into his crotch. He laughed loudly, and knew that the York Era had officially begun. Caligula rose again in the body of Charles York and his ascendance was heralded in the consumption of flesh. Long live the king.

Below him, the meat all but gone, the campers

rolled and writhed on the ground. The sounds of slurping and sucking mixed with moans of ecstasy and cries of pleasure. It was impossible to tell where one camper ended and another began. The body heat and friction rose higher and higher, resulting in what could only be described as the scent of bacon sizzling in the middle of a rippling ocean.

CHAPTER TWELVE

From the Diary of Jenny Running Bear, Camp Tum Tum Day Eleven (approximate)

Dear Diary,

Or, more accurately, dear banana leaf and berry-ink. I am writing this down as a record of my activities after leaving the camp. I have been in the jungle for approximately three days, I believe. The going was very hard at first, but I followed a small inland stream and stumbled upon a banana grove. I think they are called groves, and a few coconut trees. The bananas were fairly easy to get down, but the coconuts were a bit tougher. I managed, after many failed attempts, to get far enough up the tree and used a branch to knock a coconut down. It was wonderful.

I have made a distinct effort to never sleep in the banana grove area. I know that Charles, and his cabinet, are still in pursuit. I rest during the day and then forage at night. I've made a nice little shelter from large palm fronds and have weaved them together using other jungle materials. My ancestors would be proud. I believe that the shelter is hidden enough as to throw off the York Rich Kids Posse, at least for the time being. If they continue to eat . . . I can't even write it. If they continue the low carb diet they are on, the weight they are losing will be very rapid and they will be more mobile soon. In that case, I would rather be Sitting Bull than sitting duck. My apologies, that was a bad joke but I need all the humor I can muster right now.

Their weight loss notwithstanding, I have begun to notice some distinct physical changes myself. I have been very active, exploring this island (which I do think is uninhabited), and finding a trove of berries, nuts and the fruit I had mentioned before. If only Charles would have waited! Tommy Wheeler, and who knows who else, would still be alive. I'm concerned for them. All of them. They have taken a path that very few people in this world have ever taken and walked away from unscathed. Not even my people, who were called savages, have committed such atrocities. Mostly, though, I fear for Miles.

I know that he didn't want to take any part in what happened and I can even understand his unwillingness to tell me what Charles did to Tommy, but he needs to get out of there. I have scouted close to the camp during the evening when they are all asleep. I believe that I can get to Miles and convince him to leave with me, especially if I can show him the bounty that the land provides. The key is to go in under cover of night and be as the wind.

This past week has been rejuvenating, in a way. I've found that, when it is necessary, I can forgo the high calorie foods and actually am able to maintain a regime of physical activity. Necessity breeds!

With this newfound energy and purpose, I will be attempting to undertake my rescue mission in two days time, I believe. I have the routine for the camp mapped out pretty well. One or two more nights of watching and waiting and I will be able to liberate Miles from this godforsaken place.

JRB

***

From the Official Record of the Reign of Charles York, Prime Minister of Tum Tum Island

I can't fucking find her and its driving me mad.

I've sent multiple teams into that forest to search, and all have returned without her. One claimed he spotted her dashing through the trees, but from what I remember, she wasn't in any kind of shape to dash. How is this happening? An overweight girl in the woods has made it this long? A week? Perhaps I underestimated her. Or maybe she is dead right now. If so, I hope her last moments were painful.

She must be found and brought back to Tum Tum, dead or alive. I have to let all the campers know that Charles York doesn't fuck up. Already, I can hear their grumbles, feel their eyes on me. They're mocking me! I guarantee I will have the last laugh.

The leftovers from Tommy lasted longer than I expected. You didn't think I'd give all the meat to them that night, did you? I'm trying to ration here, remember? Freda has done a great job rationing the food and finally there's a small semblance of order. Still, we are going to need more, and I must admit something sinister. Now that I've tasted human meat . . . I want more!

It was sweeter than I thought it would be. Tender, like pork loin, but rich like filet mignon. If somehow we are rescued, I don't know if I'll be able to stop eating it. I don't think I want to stop. No. I know I want more.

One of the younger campers hurt herself the other day. It was bad. Her name is Wendy Canas, the sweet Colombian child, and her time is coming to an end. An unfortunate incident running through a field and stepping in a hole, snapping her leg, is to blame. She's in a lot of pain and, frankly, we don't have any idea what to do. Her leg is infected, and I'm going to propose removing it from her body and then using the rest of her to get us through another week. All I'm doing is following Darwinism. The strong eat the weak. The circle of life.

What to make with her? I don't know. I'll let Freda handle that, maybe some kind of meat loaf or hamburger steak. Still, Wendy will be hailed a hero and savior to us. Her death will be carried out as painlessly as possible. She'll understand. It'll make things so much easier if she does. And if she doesn't, well, then I can't promise her quick and painless.

The hardest part has been getting these pompous rich fucks organized. Everyone is so used to their maids, butlers, and credit cards that they don't even know how to do the most basic of tasks. I have crews working on a garden, some are on clean-up duty, and my personal cabinet of security remains busy maintaining order. We have a group of hunters and they are starting to get better. I've built a nice community with what I have and each day holds more and more promise. The only real thorn in my side has been Miles.

Ever since Jenny took off, he's been a sad sack of shit. His moping around is grating on my last nerve, and the other day he never left his cabin. He just stayed in there. Is he that wrapped up in Running Bear? He better not be or he's going to be mightily disappointed when he sees the plans I have for her. She questioned my authority. She'll suffer for that. I pray she's still alive. I'll speak with Miles. Maybe I can get him back in line. He's on a short leash right now.

Some exciting news to report. We found three cases of protein bars in one of the counselor's rooms. I'm holding onto them for now, until we get desperate and are out of options. I checked the nutritional value and it seems they'd be enough to sustain us all for a week, so long as each camper eats only three a day. I'll preface this by saying: I don't want to eat anyone, logistically. It is bad form. I need everyone to help make our situation sustainable. But at the same time, I'll take what I can get. If the situation becomes dire, I'll have to start ranking people in terms of importance to the community. It makes it easier when they basically volunteer themselves, like Wendy Canas.

I hope no one finds us. This truly is a paradise and can be so much better. No parents to make us feel like constant disappointments, and no assholes to remind us of the fat slobs we are. Speaking of, I'm losing a few pounds. We all are. You see that, mom and dad? Your little disappointment is getting thin! That's what you always wanted, right? Well out here, I don't have to worry about how you see me. I am everything out here. God and Satan! Hitler and FDR! I answer to no one.

But everyone will answer to me.

CHAPTER THIRTEEN

Letter Home, Day Twelve: Landish, Miles

Hello mother, hello father,

If you read this and I am no longer here, please make sure that you know how sorry I am. I'm so sorry for everything, for what we did and for Tommy and for not being able to stop. I'm not sure how much of this is being recorded by anyone else, so it may be up to me to make sure that the world knows what we've done. And Jenny, the world has to know that Jenny didn't have anything to do with it. Make sure everyone knows that.

I really should have told someone what happened to Tommy. It wasn't right but, and I hate to admit this, I was scared. Terrified. How many times have I done that sort of thing in a video game? Tons, but to have it done to someone you know, right in front of your face? It was insane. Charles just shoved the spear into Tommy again and again and again. This is what really happened: Charles York murdered Tommy Miller.

You should have seen his face. I don't think I've ever seen anyone angrier than Charles was then. His face twisted, literally, twisted in rage and he hissed. I don't even know if he realized it, but he hissed... like an animal. If I'm being truthful, I probably could have stopped him. It happened fast, but I could have stopped him from killing Tommy, I think. I was too scared, though. Imagine that, Dad! Another disappointing moment in the short, fat history of your loser son. Thanks again for this wonderful opportunity.

I held it in. I didn't even tell Jenny. It got worse, though. The night before the big meeting, Charles told me his plan. He had chosen a cabinet and was preparing to declare himself the Prime Minister of the island. I laughed; what else could I do? There was no way the campers would follow him anywhere, especially after they found out about Tommy. He gave me an idea of what he was planning, weird little hints to what the general idea was, but I refused to believe it. I mean, who would? He said that, thanks to Tommy, he would be unanimously declared leader, he would end the pangs of hunger and he would do it by telling the truth. There was no way. I took him at his word when he said he would tell the truth, but the other stuff? It had crossed my mind but I never thought he would go so far as to cook and serve another human being.

And, dear God, I ate it. I ate it! I'm sorry, mother.

I couldn't stop eating, I was so hungry. I shoved so much meat into my mouth at times I could hardly breathe and it was wonderful. I don't want to admit to it, but the taste was glorious. The texture reminded me of a pulled pork, but the taste was unlike anything I had ever had. I realize that you have hired the finest chefs on the planet and I've eaten the lunches of some of the richest families in the world, but it all paled.

Truthfully, and it tears at my heart, but it was the finest meat I had ever eaten and melted in my mouth, even if it was a bit greasy.

Physically, I'm very sore. My muscles ache and, with that said, I have to make another confession. The group of us, eating Tommy like that, fell into some kind of . . . something. I don't know what to call it, maybe group hypnosis or some kind of mob behavior. Whatever happened, it came from the meat. I swear to you, I would never do anything like this under normal conditions, but the meat was so seductive! That's the word! Chewing Tommy like that opened our eyes.

I haven't talked to anyone else yet. I don't even think the rest of the camp is up yet. Most of them are probably as sore and as weak as I am right now. Please don't be disappointed when I tell you this, mother. Dad won't be angry, probably shocked, though. I get the impression that he thought I was gay for the longest time. Regardless, I am no longer a virgin.

The meat, the feasting, it was all so erotic. I want this documented, for posterity. I know that you might not want to hear this, but it is your fault I'm in the middle of this anyway. I've had erections before. Lots of them. I've touched myself, too. It isn't like some beautiful woman was going to sleep with me, right? Not the way I looked. But it is different here, especially after Tommy.

I didn't even know her full name but, in the middle of gorging, really, gorging, we looked at each other and a switch flipped. Maybe it was Charles and Freda, who started, or the vibe in the room. I think it was the meat. It was so wrong, what we did, but we all loved it. We ALL loved it. If there is someone else writing this down and they were in that room, rest assured. They ate human flesh. They loved eating human flesh and they fucked their brains out covered in human meat grease.

I can't believe I just wrote that. We looked at each other, mouths full of meat, and it just happened. The next thing I knew we were both naked and all around us everyone else was naked. It's horrible, but it felt so good. We did it again and again; it felt like we were smashed together for hours and hours. All of us, Charles included, woke up in that room the next morning. Bodies were strewn everywhere, on top of one another. It took some time for everyone to separate themselves, the residue of the feast and other stuff made that difficult. No one spoke as we left. I'm not sure anyone had anything to say or enough saliva left to say it. Except for Charles. He told us to, "Sleep well. A new era has begun."

I know this is going to be another disappointment to you, but I cried. I slept and woke up and cried again. I'm so sorry any of this happened. I'm so sorry I couldn't stop and I'm so sorry that I'm here.

We know who to blame there, though, don't we.

The only thing I can focus on now is Jenny. Charles sent his "cabinet" out to find her. She did the bravest thing I've ever seen and ran from that room. Ran before Tommy and before the things that happened after. I'm afraid for her.

Charles is obsessed with finding her. He sees it as some kind of middle finger to his Prime Minister-ship and wants her found. I know he is still a reasonable person, though. I know it! In situations like this we all do crazy things, I'm living proof. So I've decided on a course of action: I am going to find Jenny on my own and convince her to come in. She has to be starving anyway. If she just listens, she'll see that I'm right. Charles will see that Jenny is willing to listen to him, she will be turning herself over without any violence and, most importantly, no one gets hurt! No more.

A girl, Wendy, broke her leg accidentally the other day and it doesn't look very good. Charles is pressuring her to make the big sacrifice for the camp. I don't want that to be Jenny. It can't be. I've already let her down so much.

Despite it all, I miss you. I love you both. Please try to forgive me.

Miles

Beastloaf Ingredients, a recipe from the kitchen of Freda Packer

Original recipe serves 40:

2 pounds of bread crumbs, NOT WHEAT
8 carrots, when not on a deserted island
5 ribs celery, when not on a deserted island
2.5 onions, when not on a deserted island
2.5 red bell peppers, when not on a deserted island
20 white mushrooms, when not on a deserted island
15 cloves garlic, when not on a deserted island
12.5 pounds ground Chuck or Tammy or Bob
5 tablespoons Worcestershire sauce
5 eggs, assaulted
10 teaspoons salt

Glaze Ingredients:

One Family-Size Bottle of Ketchup

Directions:

Preheat the oven to 325 degrees F. Place the vegetables, after chopping, in a blender and finely chop even further. If no veggies are available, skip that part.

Place the vegetables into the largest container you can find, and mix in the ground whomever, and egg. Add salt, black pepper, and whatever ethnic spice you fill like.

Mix gently with a wooden spoon to incorporate vegetables and egg into the meat. Gently is key, bruising the meat would result in a poor beastloaf. Pour in bread crumbs and, with your hand, gently mix in the crumbs with your fingertips, running your fingers through the chilled meat.

Form the beastloaf into whatever shape you find enjoyable. Some ideas include: bachelorette party penises, SuperBowl footballs and 3D representations of the Mona Lisa for an art gallery opening.

Place the ball of meat into the dish.

Bake in the preheated oven just until the loaf is hot.

Remove the beastloaf from the oven. Empty the family-size bottle of ketchup over the beastloaf.

Return loaf to oven, and bake until the loaf is no longer pink inside.

CHAPTER FOURTEEN

ARCHIBALD LODGE FELT the sweat drip down the back of his neck as he fidgeted with his pen. The lights above were hotter than he remembered, and, as each second ticked by, they only grew more radiant. He glanced over to his business partner, Reginald Waters, and noticed how the man appeared ill. Of course, anyone would be ill when dozens of the world's most powerful couples had you down the barrel of a gun. Archibald leaned forward into the microphone.

"I know why you have called us to gather here today, and I can assure you that everything is okay. There have been no incidents, only a failure with the satellite phone."

"How can you say everything is okay?" a man said, rising from his chair and pointing an accusing finger. "I demand to speak with my son."

Voices behind him echoed in support. Archibald felt as if a foot had been introduced to his stomach. Reginald stared at his prepared statement.

"Please, you must remain calm," Archibald said, motioning with his hand for the man to take his seat. "The well-being of your children is very important to us. Right now, they are in the care of some of the best trainers on the planet. These fine adults are the best in their fields, not only athletically, but also in culinary skills and survival tactics, not that we anticipate survival tactics will be needed. Everyone just needs to be patient."

Reginald placed a hand to his forehead as the room exploded. Shouts and demands clambered through the small meeting room. Mothers cried and fathers pounded fists. All of them wanted answers, and none were in any position to be told to "be patient." Archibald saw one of his favorite musicians walk to the front of the room where he and Reginald were situated. The rocker stopped and placed two wrinkled hands on the desk. His eyes remained hidden behind thick sunglasses and hot, smoky breath blasted Archibald's face.

"You either let me talk to my kid now, or I'm going to beat you to death with my Gibson."

"Mr. Wheeler, please have a seat. I know you must be quite worried, but trust me when I say we are working on getting the phones back on line." Archibald motioned for the rock icon to return to his seat.

The man snorted and glared at the two camp owners before turning away and stomping off. Archibald turned to his longtime friend and business partner and tried to give him a comforting smile. Only a cold line remained on Reginald's face. Archibald knew they'd been through plenty of ups and downs. Through hard work and perseverance, they'd taken a small landscaping company into one of the largest home retail stores in the world. Both being chubby kids growing up, they devoted their vast resources to combating childhood obesity and implementing dieting programs for impoverished youth. Camp Tum Tum was something different. It was a gift to their powerful friends who had kids that needed a special type of "reprogramming."

As a youth, Archibald had been cruelly nicknamed 'tum-tum' by his classmates. He'd taken a negative and turned it around into a huge positive. The cruel nickname, once used to hurt and shame, was now a camp that assisted the elite to get fit. It appeared, now, that something had gone horribly wrong. He snapped out of this brief day dream when Reginald rose up and spoke to the room with his signature, booming voice.

"Ladies and gentlemen, we thank you for your patience and understanding. Archibald and I will be taking our helicopter to the camp site and will personally check in on the situation. I can't say for certain, but I would bet that there has been an issue with the phone and we will report back personally to each one of you with a message from your child, no doubt saying how much fun they are having. If you need to worry about anything, it is whether or not your kid will want to come home after a summer of fun."

A light ripple of laughter rolled through the hall. Smiling faces replaced sour grimaces and Archibald eased back in his chair. Reginald had always been the one to put the grounds at ease. He was glad his friend had finally broken his silence.

"When will you be leaving?" a woman covered with diamonds asked.

"It is Wednesday now. We will leave on Friday, spend the weekend with the campers, and then return Sunday evening with good news and letters from your kids. Now, let us all resume our busy and successful lives. I'll be in touch."

Reginald sat back down and the two men watched the parents file out of the room. Archibald could still feel their angry glares upon him. The door closed and the pair sat in silence for a few moments, letting the reality of the situation pass.

"Well, that could have gone better," Reginald said.

"I'm glad you spoke when you did. I was about to lose the room." Archibald crumpled a piece of paper and tossed it into a trashcan nearby.

"Yeah, well I've always been the people person. I can't believe we have to fly out there. I was hoping to take my kids fishing this weekend."

"You and me both. Any other time I'd just send my assistant, but I guess this one calls for us to make an appearance. Still, it's not a terrible idea. It would be nice to show our faces and see how the place is run, a great photo-op as well."

"What do you think happened? That phone was top of the line. I know it didn't just go out."

"Who knows? Probably that massive Ukrainian bull we hired sat on it."

"The Russian?"

"Yeah, that guy. Remember when we interviewed him? He kept running into walls and he smashed the wooden chair he sat in. The guy's an accident waiting to happen."

"I hope you're right. I can't help but feel something might have happened. We did scout that island. There were no threats. No natives living there or dangerous species, other than what's normally found in a tropical forest setting. But I don't know why I have this feeling."

"Calm down. The phone broke, the kids are fine. You'll see when we get there."

"And if I'm right? If we get there and say something has happened?"

"Archibald, old friend, I don't know what could possibly happen that would be that horrible."

"I suppose you're right."

"Don't let those assholes intimidate you. Your net worth matches theirs. We run in the same circles. They aren't over us in any way, and we will not be disrespected. That said, we do owe it to worried parents to let them know their kids are all right."

"You hungry, Reg? I could go for a nice steak and a few scotches."

"Now we're on the same page."

Reginald clapped Archibald on the back and the two men walked out of the room. Archibald paused for a moment before turning off the lights to the private meeting room; a chill ran down his spine and the sickening feeling of regret settled deep in his gut. He knew there was something wrong, and a horrible surprise awaited them when their feet touched the ground of Camp Tum Tum.

He ran a hand through his thinning hair and rubbed his eyes. After a few glasses of scotch, he knew the entire outlook would change. Maybe he could convince Reginald for them to leave earlier. He really didn't want to waste his weekend being pawed and slobbered over by fat children.

"Archie, come on. My stomach is rumbling!"

Archibald shut the door and headed down to the open doors of the limousine. His thoughts changed from despairing the fate of those campers to which steak he would order—the prime filet or the Wagyu rib cap. He smiled. It was great being rich.

***

The blood ran down Jenny's arm, hot and smelling of iron, as she plunged the sharpened branch deeper into the wiggling jowl of Bernard Shyer. He gurgled, and she quickly clasped a hand over his mouth to muffle any feeble attempt at a scream. She felt his teeth try to bite her hand away, but shock had set in and his nibble lacked enthusiasm.

He went limp, and Jenny managed to ease his massive body down. She contemplated dragging him and trying to hide the corpse, but realized that would be an arduous task. Though she'd found enough food to survive on, it still left her weak. Hauling three hundred pounds of limp meat would be a chore for even a trained bodybuilder. She decided against it and continued her way to Miles' cabin.

She hadn't wanted to kill Bernard, but he'd left her no choice. As soon as she'd appeared from the thick brush, he spotted her. Fortunately, he was busy relieving himself onto a tree and her sudden appearance had shocked him. She'd seen his mouth open, and knew a scream was on the way. It had been a blur—the attack. The murder. Was she any better than Charles? She didn't feel bad about what she'd done, justifying it as necessity in the name of survival. Still, someone would stumble upon the body, and the alarm would sound. Time was running out. She had to find Miles and convince him to run away with her, deep into the forest.

There was a cave she'd taken residence in that provided ample access to fruit and clean drinking water. They could live there for as long as needed, and as the days went by, she believed help would arrive. They weren't no-bodies. Their parents were powerful people, and she couldn't imagine they'd go a long period of time without hearing word from their kids. Unless . . .

Unless this was all just some sick experiment. Like reality television, but worse. Were they put here on purpose and forced into a situation where they'd have to do the most heinous things imaginable to survive? Could it be their parents were ashamed of them and banished them to a living Hell? A single tear rolled down Jenny's mud-stained face, but she refused to wipe it away. In the tradition of her people, she'd wear it like a badge of honor. She'd earned that tear, and hoped there wouldn't be more by the end of the night.

Torches lit a trail for her and the cabins stood dark and silent. The hour was late and she knew the campers were asleep. She'd scouted the camps for a few nights now, and noticed two or three campers usually walked around on patrol, operating on some kind of shift. Stumbling upon poor Bernard had been a surprise she hadn't anticipated, but luckily it was one that hadn't cost her life. The other two guards she'd known were absent, and she guessed were busy slumbering somewhere, or blowing one another. Who knows what went on in this place after hours.

She stuck to the shadows, pressing against the wood walls and keeping low. A predatory sense washed over her, and she became one with the night. Her breath was the gentle wind. Her steps were light, yet powerful, like the wolf. The sharp stick was at the ready, and it had tasted blood once tonight. It would taste blood a hundred times if it meant getting what she came for.

Nothing would stop her.

***

Miles scribbled the final words into his journal

and closed the book. He sighed and parted his hair with moist hands. Pangs of indigestion hit him like thunderous fists delivered by a prize fighter. The girl, Wendy, had been delicious.

Charles had informed the camp that she'd died from the infection, but Miles knew the truth. He was there when the pillow was placed over her face, and her death throes became pathetic flaps and flings as the life faded from her. They'd had a viewing for her and everything, and instead of being wheeled to her grave, she was maneuvered into the kitchen and under the culinary skills of Freda. Miles had to admit, Freda was a damn fine cook, and that night, in Wendy's honor, the entire population dined on Wendy-burger steaks with caramelized onions and this wonderful sauce concocted from tomato sauce and some kind of spice that reminded him of curry—or was it cumin?

"What the fuck is wrong with me?" He brushed off the contents of the desk in one fell swoop.

He was a cannibal. The only cannibals he'd known were deformed freaks from movies, or tribal people deep in the Amazon. He wasn't one of them. At least, he didn't think so. Surprisingly, he laughed at the realization that he resembled a tribesman lost in the forest more than he thought. How would he adjust back to normal life? Could he? Who was he kidding, what normal life could he go back to?

When help arrived, and he was sure it would, they'd lock the entire camp up in the loony bin. A camp full of cannibals. He wished he was a better writer. The idea for this would make a great book.

He stripped off his shirt and looked at his body in the mirror. It was still lumpy and imperfect, but he'd definitely lost quite a bit of weight. Maybe there was something to the no-carb fad he'd been reading about. When he got home—if he got home—he was sticking to high proteins and veggies. He'd have to replace his main source of protein with a more public-friendly variety, but he'd learn to get used to it. What choice did he have?

Shutting off the lamp, he climbed into bed and pulled the covers up to his chin. It got cold at night here. For a tropical island, it sure had a weird climate. The sounds of night serenaded him, but one sound stood out from the rest—the sound of feet creaking on weather-worn boards outside his door. The door handle rattled, causing Miles to roll out of bed and make his way to the door.

He was hoping it wasn't the girl he'd hooked up with at the orgy. The sex-crazed lunatic had rubbed him raw for the past couple days, and he didn't think he had enough stamina—or skin—for another round with her.

He flung open the door. "Listen, I'm tired. I'm sore. I'm sorry, but tonight ain't—"

Jenny's sad brown eyes nearly took his breath away.

"Jesus Christ, Jenny? Oh my God." He hugged her and she hugged back just as tight. "Quick, get in. Has anyone seen you?"

She walked past him and sat on the bed. He looked out the door and scanned the area before closing it. The only light cast in the room was from the moon through a solitary window. He'd keep all the lights off to avoid suspicion.

"Jenny, you're bleeding?" Miles had been so excited by her, that he hadn't noticed the dried blood streaked across her face, clothes, and arm.

Her clothes were stained green and brown, but what was most noticeable was how baggy they appeared on her much thinner frame. She looked good. Tired, but healthy.

"It's . . . not mine." Her voice was breathless and her eyes shimmered.

"Not yours? I don't understand."

"It's Bernard's. Please don't be mad. I had to do it. He spotted me when I got into the camp and would have blown my cover. I had to silence him."

"I'm not mad. I don't care about anyone here. This entire camp has gone crazy, and I'm embarrassed to admit that I've gotten wrapped up in it. What's the term they use for it? Herd mentality? I think that's it. Still, I have no excuse."

"Miles, we can talk when we get someplace safe."

"Like where? Where is safe?"

"I've found a spot. A cave far away from here and away from the prying eyes and savagery of Charles York and this joke of a regime. We can hide there and start a life together until the rescue party comes."

"If I leave with you, Jenny, they will only look for us harder. Right now Charles thinks you're dead, and we've scaled back on the time and people looking for you. They'd hunt us like animals, and that's how we'd live."

"So what are you saying? Did I just waste my time coming here?" Her face flushed red and her eyes transformed into shimmering pools.

"No, I'm not saying that at all. But we need to think this through. If you were to let me know where this cave was, then you could stay there safe and when the rescue party arrives, I'll let them know."

"Perhaps, but how do I know I can trust you?

You've taken to this lifestyle a little easier than I could have ever thought."

Miles reeled at the comment. She was right, though. He'd had a chance to stand up for himself and to York in front of the entire camp, and instead chosen to do nothing. Burning tears welled behind his eyes, and he blinked, allowing them to spill over his round face. He couldn't face her. Her eyes bore into him, casting shame. It wasn't fair. He'd never been put in a situation like this and had no idea how he would have reacted. He chose survival over her, and he owed her that explanation.

"I . . . was scared. That's why I did this. You weren't there in the woods that day when Charles killed Tommy. Just ran him through like he was nothing but an animal. I thought others would rally against him, but instead they joined him and his new ideals. I was horribly outnumbered and knew if I opposed him, I'd end up like Tommy—a huge pile of meat for the camp to feast on. So I chose to survive over running with you, and I'm so very sorry." The tears ran like a burst dam.

She embraced him in a hug, and he cried into her shirt, breathing in the smells of someone living in the woods for a long period of time. But behind all the earthy aromas, the smell of her perfume lingered, and he couldn't help but to allow a smile to cross his face.

He brought his head up and kissed her. Light at first, but growing in passion as each second ticked by. Surges of electricity went through his body as the wet sensation of tongues and lips met. Time froze, leaving only him and her in this one perfect moment. They parted, and a string of saliva trailed from their mouths.

"I've wanted to do that from the day I met you," he said.

"Me too." She paused. "Please, let's leave. Come with me tonight and we can live out the rest of the time here in peace."

"I can't Jenny, but tell me where you are and I'll make sure they find you when help arrives."

"Okay, you know the stream that cuts through the woods? Follow it to the east and you'll come across a large pool of water. It's a long walk, so it will take a while to get there. There's an outcrop of rocks to the west and an opening just large enough to squeeze through. You'll see the banana and coconut debris on the ground in front of it. Please, don't leave me."

"I won't. I never will."

They kissed again, and hugged. Jenny started to cry and Miles joined her. They'd been reunited, and cruel fate was going to part them again, hopefully not for long. He walked her to the door and opened it slowly, peering out into the tranquil night. There was no one.

"Be safe, Miles," she said, and left the cabin.

He stood in the doorway and watched her go. Shadows appeared around the other cabins, and he thought his eyes were playing tricks on him. Jenny screamed and his blood iced. She'd been caught. It was a trap all along.

***

Miles ran from his cabin as fast as his stubby legs would carry him. The shouts and hoots from the fellow campers grew more intense, and he knew things were going to spiral from bad to much worse.

He pushed through the ring of fatties who blocked his vision from the spectacle that transfixed them. His fears were confirmed. Jenny was on her knees, each arm held by Melton and Clarence. Charles paced in front on her, twirling the javelin like a baton. Jenny's face was one of terror. Her eyes were wide with fright and her chin trembled. Miles stood motionless.

"Jenny Running Bear, you are hereby charged with the murder of Bernard Shyer and treason in the first degree. The punishment for these crimes is death, as set by me, The Prime Minister of Tum Tum. You are not allowed to plead innocent, as there is no trial. Your fate is sealed. Your choice is to die by having your throat slit or suffocation. Which would you like?"

"No!" Miles ran forward and whipped Charles around. "You can't do this to her!"

"Well, it seems my second-in-command has joined the traitor. I can't say I'm surprised, but I'm still very disappointed. Maybe you'd like to join her and share the punishment?"

"You monster! You can't. I won't let you!"

A meaty fist flew through the air, connecting with Miles and sending him to the ground. His vision blurred and blood poured down his face. The fuzzy image of Clarence stood over him, begging Miles to get back on his feet so he could send him back down.

Miles felt woozy, and everything appeared to blur around him. He blacked-out for a second and came back. He attempted to stand, but felt his legs give out from underneath. Miles crashed back to the ground where he remained.

"Such a shame, Miles. We could have had something great here, and you could have been a part of it." Charles pointed to one of the campers and motioned him toward the injured Miles. "Raise his head up and point it at her. I want him to watch this."

The campers did as told, grabbing Miles by the hair and bending his neck back. Miles' eyes focused on Jenny, who mouthed back something he couldn't discern.

"Jenny, I'm sorry," Miles said weakly, spitting out blood.

"Not as sorry as she is," Charles said, and plunged the javelin into Jenny's throat.

Miles screamed and thrashed as the camper sat on him, keeping him on the ground. Jenny grabbed her throat and gargled as thick globs of crimson blood escaped her hands and flowed to the ground. Her eyes bugged out and tears ran from them as she pitched forward and spasmed violently. Soon, her body was still and Charles held the javelin high.

"Jenny Running Bear, murderer and traitor, is dead! Long live order and long live Tum Tum!"

"Long live Charles!" A chorus of voices rang from the crowd in unison.

Charles turned to his security team. "Take her to Freda. I want her roasted whole and served up for a feast tomorrow."

The pair gripped Jenny by her feet and dragged her away. Miles captured a glimpse of her wide, dead eyes staring back at him. The image was replaced by Charles' boot. The campers released Miles and Charles forced his head down to the ground.

"You picked the wrong team," Charles said, and raised the javelin up.

Miles waited for the tip to jab through his skull. The blunt end connected with the side of his head, and the world went black.

Charles looked down at his unconscious and disgraced Vice Prime Minister with disgust.

"Throw him in the cooler, but I want him alive. Give him something to wear if need be, but I want him to live through the feast tomorrow. He will eat the flesh of the one he helped betray us, and then his flesh will sustain us when hers is gone."

"To Charles, Prime Minister of Tum Tum!" The crowd called out again in jubilation.

Miles heard nothing as his limp body was dragged away.

CHAPTER FIFTEEN

MILES HUGGED HIMSELF and ran the events of the past fifteen minutes over and over again in his mind. He sighed and his breath crystallized in a cloud in front of his face. He stamped his feet and looked around the large, walk-in freezer. The small, dim light from the single overhead at the front of the cooler didn't illuminate much. It didn't cut into the gloom. Miles ran his hand across the cold, metallic wall looking for the switches that would turn on the rest of the lights in the giant ice box. As far as Miles knew, it had been pretty empty since the campers had eaten everything in sight on that first day, but with Charles' new laws, who knew what could end up in here.

Miles rubbed his hands together and blew on them before going back to hugging himself. What the dim lights did show, though, was the thermometer where the temperature of the freezer hovered just at freezing, it being an effective machine. Miles was dressed warmly, as far as normal circumstances go, but he knew that he wouldn't last long, however long that may be. The past fifteen minutes changed everything, though, and Miles didn't have a plan for the next fifteen.

He remembers Jenny coming to get him and he

couldn't believe what he was seeing. Jenny looked good! He managed to formulate a plan, things were still fuzzy, before anything could happen, the light blazed on and Charles and the Cabinet had her cornered. They grabbed Jenny and Miles moved to help. The next thing he saw was Charles with the butt of the javelin and, bam, that was it. Stars and unicorns. He vaguely remembered stumbling into the big walk-in freezer. When he hit the cold, Miles shook off a good deal of Charles' blow leading up to this point: looking for the lights.

Miles could only run his hand along the metallic wall in small stints; the freezing aluminum was painful to the touch after prolonged exposure. Eventually, Miles did find the bank of switches. He flipped them with a triumphant cry and spun around, eager to get a better idea of what he was facing here.

He instantly wished that the light switch had never been found or malfunctioned. What lay before Miles was a horror that he could never even have imagined, prior to the events at Camp Tum Tum, but as he stood, staring, it made an odd kind of sense.

If mental health professionals had been there, in that freezer, there would have been a consensus pinpointing the moment of Miles Landish's psychotic break. It occurred immediately after finding the lights and spinning around to find his fellow campers suspended from the ceiling.

Miles' breath shot out, visibly, in little gasps as he took in the scene. Suspended off the floor of the freezer, hanging from large meat hooks, were several Camp Tum Tum campers. They hung there, frozen in time and literally iced over, waiting for Freda Packer's butcher knife and the hungry, living residents of the camp. In front, Miles recognized her . . . the girl, with the tits. He was slightly ashamed to admit he didn't remember her name, but the situation was dire enough to push that out his mind. He decided to call her Elsie, he'd always liked that name for some reason. She still looked . . . not alive, but, functional.

Miles stepped forward and slowly reached out to Elsie. His hand shook from the cold, from fear, from insanity as he stretched. Miles stepped forward again and, before he could reach Elsie, his foot slipped backwards and he tumbled into the dead girl.

Miles planted face first into her crotch and fell to the floor, landing with a thud. He moaned in pain. Above him, Elsie had begun to swing back and forth from the force of Miles' blow she connected with another camper. Soon, the room was filled with chubby corpses, hanging from meat hooks, banging into one another. It sounded like sausage nunchucks slapping into one another to Miles and the momentum of the bodies ensured that they would play this out until the laws of physics said they could stop.

Miles' father had one of those never-ending metal ball things on his desk at home. If you took one end and let it go, it would smack into the row of hanging metal balls and the ball at the opposite end would shoot off and then come crashing down. It was perpetual motion and Miles could sit and watch if for hours, if he had brought enough snacks. Miles watched the bodies slam into one another, back and forth, and smiled. It reminded him of home.

Eventually, Miles looked down to see what had caused him to slip. Beneath each of the campers, a small frozen pool of blood spread out. From Miles' limited hunting/butchering/food preparation knowledge, the blood needed to be drained before the meat could be prepared and, in the haste to get these campers ready, they must not have been allowed to drain completely. Miles looked back up to his swinging roommates and smiled again. That was very logical.

The cold worsened and, even in the middle of a complete breakdown, Miles realized that he had to do something or he would freeze to death. Unfortunately, the frozen campers were all naked. Unfortunate in one sense because Miles could not use their clothes, but in the other sense that each of them were morbidly obese, the worst of the lot at Camp Tum Tum. Charles must have made his decisions for consumption or not based on health risk factors of the various campers or what kind of effort they could lend to the collective. Miles had to give it to Charles, for evil despots, he was a pretty smart one.

Although the temperature didn't drop in the freezer, Miles' core body temperature dipped dangerously low. Faced with freezing to death, Miles resolved to do the only thing he could.

Beginning with Elsie, he managed to wrench her off the hook and the girl's corpse crashed to the floor of the freezer. Not quite frozen enough to shatter, the body lay there awkwardly propped up on an elbow. Taking a deep breath, Miles knelt down and rolled Elsie over, exposing her back. Using his nearly-numb fingers, Miles dug into the long wound caused by the meat hook and gravity. No matter how much he pried, his fingers could find no purchase under Elsie's skin. Frustrated, Miles thumped down to the floor. He rolled over, ready for a tantrum unlike any the world had seen before when he heard metal click against metal.

Slowly, Miles sat up. Looking down, his lap was barely visible, so he ran his hand underneath the blubber overtaking the top of his pants and his hand felt a large, metal belt buckle. While he was out, Charles' goons had dressed him. He would already be dead if in his pajamas and bare feet, and they had used his belt with the only thing that could save him right now: the oversized belt buckle that he had to buy in order to keep the waist of his sixty inch pants up and not around his ankles. Elated, Miles fumbled with the belt and buckle momentarily until he got it off.

He held the buckle up, large, oval-shaped, made of nickel and sporting a big, metal hook for looping into punctured leather, Miles now had the implement he needed to get the job done.

Like peeling an orange, he was able to pry Elsie's skin away from her chilled muscle with a great deal of effort. Stopping and starting, due to the extreme temperatures and fatigue, Miles managed to wrench the skin from Elsie's body, mostly intact. It was cold and stiff to the touch but, as Miles worked with it, his own body heat softened the hide. Rubbing it down with his leather belt wrapped around his fist softened it even more.

Elsie was smaller than Miles, so her skin functioned like a reverse-hooded Snuggie. Normally, wearing the skin of another human being would turn Miles' stomach, but after what he had seen, and done, in the past few days, nothing was beyond the pale. The Elsie Snuggie, or Elsggie, helped to fight a bit of the chill, but Miles' predicament would take more than a thin layer of camper. He turned to the other bodies, still gently swinging, and remembered what his mother would say before he left for school on chilly winter mornings. She would call out, "Layers, Miley! Dress in layers!" Miles's mother was very wise.

Miles wasn't sure how much time it took to skin the entire complement of campers, but knew that each layer of greasy, fatty skin he laid on top of himself, the warmer he became. First the buckle, then the belt over and over again. Minutes turned into hours, hours into more hours. Miles wasn't sure. He suspected he dozed off a few times before finishing the task.

The skinless campers lay, one on top of the other, at the rear of the cooler, their red, well-marbled muscle gleaming in the soft freezer lights. Miles, huddled under layers of skin, woke up from another of the frequent naps that punctuated his isolation.

His stomach rumbled.

Miles looked down as if some kind of physical change would be evident due to the loudness of the tummy grumbling and was surprised to find his large, flabby stomach in its usual state.

Miles' stomach rumbled again, louder, reverberating off the metal walls of the freezer. He looked around the room knowing full well what decision he was about to come to, but wanting an out. No errant buckets of ice cream, or sides of beef hidden in a shadowy corner made themselves apparent so, inevitably, Miles turned to the glistening red campers, stacked neatly a few feet away.

Miles stood awkwardly, balancing the pile of fatty hides he was wearing, and shambled over to the stack. He knelt and reached a hand out to the bottom corpse, going to his trusted guinea pig, Elsie.

Miles had heard of steak tar tar before and had even had a penchant for eel-based sushi. This was new, though. He stroked the muscle of Elsie's forearm, unsure of just how to approach this latest atrocity. Without further thought, he dug in and snapped off a piece of the girl's muscle.

Miles was shocked by the sound it made, literally snapping off. He smiled and regarded the thin piece of fatty muscle. Between the sound, the color and the psychotic break, he thought that he was holding a Slim Jim. Miles laughed out loud. He croaked out that laugh, like fish scales on sandpaper, and realized that his throat was incredibly dry as well. Still holding the sliver of Elsie, Miles stood and, noticing the pool of frozen blood all over again, headed that way.

He knelt down and, digging his fingers into the frozen pool, pulled out a handful of frozen blood the consistency of a slushie. Miles laughed again. What luck!

"What a great day," he said, "I can't believe I found a whole stack of Slim Jims and cherry Slurpees hiding in this freezer!"

Miles turned to the campers stacked at the rear of the freezer.

"Thanks, guys!" he called out, and shoved the Elsie stick in his mouth. He chewed happily, dipping from time to time to his cupped hand to suck a little blood slush to wash it all down with.

Miles sat back against the wall and snuggled in his Elsggie, skin suits and Really Fat Kid Hoodie. He chomped away on slivers of meat and schlurped the frozen blood with a smile on his face. Better yet, he had a great conversation with his parents over the meal. He thought that, when he went back for seconds, thirds and fourths, he might also have a great conversation and trade recipes with Joseph Mengele and Wolfgang Puck.

He might even start that poetry chapbook he'd been meaning to write. Who knew? Today was coming up Miles!

***

The following is a transcription of poetic verse found scrawled on the walls of the walk-in freezer. This transcript is based on photographs taken by The National Guard prior to Operation: Wiener Roast.

It is generally assumed that these words were etched into the wall using the same implement that Miles Landish used to liberate the hides from their owners.

Verse #1
Roses are red
Violets are blue
Chili is good with crackers

Verse #2
Jenny
Jenny
Jenny
Jenny

Verse #3
Never again
Will I see
Another sun.
Never again
Will she be
Free to run.

Verse #4
Hollow, empty.
Not lack of food.
My soul is gone.
Another pit,
Another hole.
I've eaten my soul.

CHAPTER SIXTEEN

CAPTAIN DILLON JACOBS landed the chopper down as smooth as he could, but a sudden gust from the north caused the bird to sail on him just a bit. He corrected, expertly, and began the descent down to the helipad.

"You two might want to hold on to your drinks, or finish them." He turned back to Archibald and Reginald who were slowly nursing vodkas on the rocks with a lime twist.

"Nonsense," Archibald said. "This is sipping vodka, not a shot at some frat house."

"Agreed," Reginald added, and took a slow pull from his glass.

"Okay, I tried to warn you."

The chopped set down with an abrupt jerk, and Jacobs muffled a laugh as the two drinks flew in the air, pouring their contents onto the two moguls. Hands produced handkerchiefs and mouths produced curse words.

"Damnit, Jacobs. Why didn't you warn us?" Reginald dappled his face, which was now a shade darker.

"You're right, sir. Entirely my fault."

Jacobs wondered how much longer he was going

to put up with this shit. A retired Navy Seal, he took this cushy job as a personal pilot because it paid extremely well, and there was never any doubt if he'd come back home that night. But the two assholes who hired him were pushy, bitter men who put on a front of caring for others, when in fact all they cared for were their bottom line. He'd been required to sign a form stating he'd be sued and possibly jailed for repeating any conversations he'd heard in private to the public. They didn't have to worry about him. He only cared about getting home to Gracie, the daughter who'd grown up without him while he was busy fighting a worthless war in the Middle East. Archibald and Reginald were pains, but at least he didn't have to worry about one strapping a bomb to their chest and running at him.

Only throwing an empty rocks glass at his head.

"Really, Jacobs. A little head's up would have been nice. This suit cost more than your salary." Archibald wiped furiously at his sleeve.

"Well, at least vodka is clear," Jacobs said, and powered off the chopper.

The two men sat stunned at the sudden quip by their employee. Jacobs removed his .45 from his hip and checked the clip and clicked off the safety. He had no idea why this trip was needed, but the tension and hushed conversation during the flight had his suspicions on guard.

"What is that for?" Archibald asked, eyeing the weapon.

"No need to worry, Mr. Archibald. This is only for protection just in case. It will not leave my hip unless absolutely necessary."

Jacobs exited the chopper and helped the two men

out of the now-still whirly bird. Humid air carried by a sharp breeze slapped his face, and the smell of earth and salt filled his nostrils. Warm sun dripped down overhead, and he smiled. The place was gorgeous. No wonder the kids hadn't called anyone, he figured. It was a paradise!

"The camp is a couple of miles from here, and there is a paved path for us to follow. There should be a golf cart for us to use, but I don't see it. Great. We'll have to walk." Reginald stared around, looking for the cart that wasn't there.

"Do you want me to walk to the camp, sirs? You both can stay here and wait for me to return."

"No, Jacobs. It's a good idea, but we really should be there to see it ourselves and speak with the counselors. It's only two miles; we should be able to walk it just fine." Archibald said. Reginald didn't look so sure.

"Okay, I'll lead the way," Jacobs said, and the trio set off down the trail toward the camp.

He kept his laughter in check as the sounds of wheezing and stumbling filled his ears. The two fat cats weren't used to any kind of walking that wasn't paved or air conditioned. Sounds of slapping cracked out like firecrackers as the two men swatted mosquitoes and stinging flies. Jacobs didn't feel any bites and wondered if the attacking insects were merely psychosomatic.

It took nearly an hour to reach the camp—Jacobs knew he could have shaved a good thirty minutes off that time if allowed to have gone alone—and when they did, the place appeared deserted.

"This isn't good," Reginald said, and Archibald nodded.

"Hello! Anybody here?" Jacobs called out. His voice echoed and then faded.

"Should we split up and look for someone?" Archibald said.

"Sir, I'd prefer it if you stuck with me." Jacobs drew his gun and positioned it at the ready. "Come, let's make a sweep and then get back to the helicopter."

They walked the camp, peering into a few cabins that were unlocked. The rooms were clean and appeared to have been used. A stack of clean, white stones captured Jacobs' attention as they made their way to the dining area. He knelt down, and realized he was looking at bones. Hidden underneath were three skulls stripped clean of any muscle or tissue.

"What is it?" Archibald asked, as he walked in for a closer look. Reginald kept his distance.

"Sir, we need to get back to the chopper, now."

A rush of wind flew past Jacobs' head, quick and sudden like a swooping bird. He turned in the direction it passed, and his eyes went wide as Archibald held the arrow that was firmly planted in his chest. Two more arrows shot forth, and struck the man, whose eyes bulged and a slivered trail of blood seeped from the corner of his mouth. Reginald covered his mouth in shock as his friend pitched forward.

Jacobs whipped around but couldn't believe his eyes. Four fat kids, who he assumed to be campers, stood proudly with bow and arrows drawn. Each wore shredded shirts that bore the insignia of Camp Tum Tum. Their round faces were smeared with a dark substance to give them a menacing look. Jacobs aimed his .45.

"Drop your weapons immediately, or I'll shoot!"

One of the kids prepped another arrow and Jacobs pled silently for the kid to not go through with this.

"Kid, if you aim that at me, I will fucking shoot you. Please, don't try me."

The kid didn't listen, and the moment the camper brought the arrow up, Jacobs sent a bullet flying his way, crashing into the camper's chest and dropping him. The three others dropped their bow and arrows and ran off, disappearing from sight.

"Sir, we need to go, now!"

Jacobs grabbed Reginald's arm to get him moving, but the business man was firmly planted over his dead friend. A sharp pain struck Jacobs in the arm, and he looked down to see the shaft of an arrow sticking out of him. He pulled it out, it slid easily, and threw it to the ground. Reginald still hadn't moved, and Jacobs couldn't wait for him.

A chorus of screams erupted, and from the far end of the dining hall, a stampede of campers revealed themselves. Knives, javelins, and sharpened pieces of wood were their weapons, and they washed over the still Reginald like a butchering wave. The man screamed as the campers used weapons and teeth to put a quick end to his life. Jacobs ran to the helicopter.

His arm bled profusely, but he didn't dare stop as he sprinted up the trail to the helipad. His lungs burned and his vision faded to black a few times, but he pressed on. The gun dangled from his good hand, and he knew there were 12 bullets left in the clip. He'd use one on himself before getting butchered like Reginald had.

He burst through the canopy and stopped, dumbfounded at the sight in front of the chopper. At least a dozen campers stood proudly, weapons drawn. One in particular stood at the front wearing a ridiculous looking headdress of feathers. A necklace of bones lay draped around his thick neck.

"Kid, get out of my way. I have enough bullets to put you all down and I'll do it."

"How dare you address me as such," Charles said, slamming his javelin into the ground. The rest of the campers stomped their feet in unison. "Why do you come here and disturb our paradise?"

"Paradise? Jesus Christ, what the hell happened? You kids were just here for summer camp."

"Were we? Or were we sent here for a greater purpose? Maybe to find out just who we are and what we are capable of when left to fend for ourselves."

"You killed the camp founders! You've clearly killed others. Why?"

"Simple. We needed to eat." Charles smiled a wicked grin. "And with their meat, and yours, we'll be able to survive for a long time."

The attack came from behind, and Jacobs should have been ready for it. All the years of military training failed as the situation he'd been plunged in had left him rattled. This was nothing like Iraq or Afghanistan. This was beyond his comprehension.

The bolts struck him in the back, and he pitched forward. A camper ran toward him, and Jacobs fired off a round into his chest, dropping him. A path opened up for the helicopter, and he had a small window. It would take ten minutes for the chopper to prime itself for flight, and he knew the odds of him leaving alive were low. The iron taste of blood was already filling his mouth, and he knew vital organs had been pierced.

He lurched forward and fired off a few more rounds of covering fire. He tried to locate the boy he assumed to be the leader, but the kid was nowhere in sight. The door to the chopper swung open as arrows bounced off the metal around him. One struck him in the leg, and he cried out. He lunged for the control panel and grabbed the radio, depressing the button to speak.

"Mayday, mayday! This is Chopper 072583 requesting emergency assistance. Multiple casualties. Under attack! Help!"

There was a crackle of static on the other end, but no response. He tried again.

"Help, please. They're killing us—"

The javelin struck through his stomach, and he knew it was over. It had to have been the leader, that fat punk who stared at him so confidently. His only regret in life was not putting a bullet between the kid's eyes when he had the chance.

Jacobs spit up blood and gasped as the javelin came down again. And again. His world was quickly fading to black, and breathing was becoming difficult.

"*Chopper 072583 we read you. Emergency team dispatched. Over.*"

Jacobs smiled. His message had gone through and someone would be held accountable for what transpired here. He thought of his wife and child, and begged God to look out for them since he wouldn't be around. His last thoughts were of them as the javelin came done a final time, piercing his heart, and sending him into eternal blackness.

***

From *The Weekly Standard:*

3 AMERICAN CASUALTIES RESULT IN ISLAND ASSAULT

St. Thomas, U.S. Virgin Islands—Most cartographers assumed the small island of St. Nimis, just a scant 10 kilometers off the northern tip of St. Thomas, was uninhabited. In an unprecedented turn of events, three American citizens lost their lives after being set upon by what can only be described as an unknown tribe of indigenous peoples. United States diet billionaires, Archibald Lodge and Reginald Waters, as well as their helicopter pilot were attacked and killed by what the United States Government is now calling the Nimis Tribe. Prior to his death, the helicopter pilot managed to radio for help and a group of National Guardsmen, activated by the President and Governor Cartegna, were dispatched to the area.

It is still unclear exactly what Lodge and Waters were doing on the small island, but records indicate that they had purchased the parcel of land, barely four square kilometers, a few years ago. The duo has had a great deal of success in creating fitness camps and weight loss collectives over the years so it would stand to reason that St. Nimis would play a role in that business model as well. Debbie Simmons, assistant to Lodge and one of the first beneficiaries of the pair's *Total Weight: Loss! System*, said that she had no idea why the billionaire entrepreneurs were interested in St. Nimi, but "if I know . . . knew them, and I do . . . did, they were there to improve the life of an obese child. That was their goal in life. They shared that."

The attack by the Nimis, and the death of three American citizens, was not taken lightly by the State Department. A pre-dawn excursion was sent to the small island and, although reports are sketchy, we are getting word that the threat has been "neutralized." This was evident even from St. Thomas as large fires could be seen blazing on the little island to the south after a small contingent of jets were dispatched from the Naval Air Station in Key West, Florida.

The National Guard has not been recalled from the island, but reports from St. Thomas have indicated that a transport has made its way from St. Nimi to St. Thomas. Local police presence at the harbor has been doubled and, if the reports from inside the campaign that we have are correct, a least one Nimi has survived the military action and is en route to the U.S. mainland.

—Trico Busser, special to *The Weekly Standard*

***

TACAIR Request Form

Requesting Officer: Major Lance Brigmann

Heading: East/South East

Distance: 1026 nautical miles

Target Elevation: 200 feet above sea level

Target Description: Total island target area minus beach head encampment of platoon. Complete coverage, including buildings and surrounding foliage.

Target Location: 18° 20" N x 64° 70" W

Type Mark: Code: Beacon Set

Location of Friendlies: All friendlies have been evacuated. Proceed with extreme prejudice.

Position Marked by: Four low buildings and surrounding foliage. Beacon centralized.

Egress: Return, West/North West to NAS

Remarks (As Appropriate): Approximately twenty-five island inhabitants encountered, but they are believed to be a neutralized threat at this point. Conduct air support under the assumption that threat has not been neutralized. One friendly, found in a walk-in freezer, has been transported to St. Thomas en route to Key West suffering from severe hypothermia, delusions and a strange combination of malnutrition and obesity. Name unknown, he was speaking English fluently but unable to answer direct questioning. Assumption is that he is a U.S. or Canadian national.

Air support at this time is Code: Nyquil. If visual contact is made with inhabitants, report immediately to NAS Debriefing, Colonel Sanders.

Time on Target (TOT): 27 minutes, NAS to cords.

Additional Notes, Brigmann, BRASS EYES ONLY.

Sirs, I felt the need to communicate exactly what

we encountered on that island. The buildings and living areas looked like animal caves. Excrement and body parts littered the main dining area and the smell, sirs, the only way I can describe that smell is to imagine a cow ate a turd the size of a Hyundai and died. When it died, the cow shit out the shit it ate and all of it decomposed together. That is all that came to mind and it is accurate. This may be wrong, only time will tell, but it looked as if the targets were eating other human beings. In our door to door, we encountered and neutralized a good fifteen bogies. Each of them was naked, more or less, and following the orders of one they called 'Charles.' Obviously, a tactical advantage would be gained by taking out their leader, but the others were devoted to him. Any tactical pursuit of this Charles resulted in one or more of the other bogies sacrificing themselves to protect him.

Their weapons consisted of sporting javelins, archery-range level bows and arrows and, believe it or not, human femurs wielded as clubs. It was a bizarre site. Private Colson sustained a minor injury when a bogie shot an arrow into his thigh. It is just a flesh wound and he is being treated on the beach.

We finally managed to pin down Charles with three bogies. He threw down his weapon, a javelin, and ripped off what little clothing he had on. It was a horrible sight, but a female bogie he called 'Freda' dropped to her knees, despite me and seven members of my platoon pointed our weapons at them. She began to fellate Charles and he raised his arms to the sky, screaming. Let me note, and this will sound odd, that each one of these bogies was extremely overweight. I've never seen anything like this in my life. All of them were really fat and we just couldn't get over all that stuff flinging around. Whenever they moved or attacked, big slabs of meat would swing and slap against one another. There was no way they could sneak through the underbrush, much less mount a significant attack.

Before Freda finished with Charles, we neutralized that threat.

In our search, we did find one friendly. He was unable to tell us his name and was located in a walk-in freezer. We can only assume he was the camp's next meal. He managed to survive by wearing the skins of other dead bogies. He is on a transport to NAS.

At this time, I would like to respectfully request a transfer to North Dakota.

***

Clinical Appraisal and DSM-IV Diagnosis: Landish, Miles

The information available for Miles is limited to a series of discussions beginning with his arrival in St. Thomas and through the reunion with his parents. His Five Axis Diagnosis, as indicated using the American Psychological Association's DSM-IV-TR (2000) follows.

Axis I: Clinical Disorders

Other Conditions That May Be a focus of Clinical Attention

Diagnostic Code DSM-IV Name

295.30 Paranoid Type Schizophrenia—Miles is suffering from delusions, bouts of disorganized speech and negative symptoms including affective flattening as evidenced in his interview (and with more observation, possibly alogia). He is also experiencing social dysfunction as evidenced by the inability to speak in coherent sentences and we project, later in life, the effects of what Miles needed to do to survive on that island and in that freezer to span a great deal of time. The duration of the symptoms will be over the course of many years. Although the information is scant, ruling out schizoaffective and mood disorders is recommended here since, in the interviews, Miles manifested major depressive, manic or mixed episodes of multiple durations. He also seems to be preoccupied with eating meat, as any malnourished individual would. In these interviews, Miles has never, once, indicated the extent of what he did on the island. The National Guard reports are scant as well. We can only hope, in time, that he will be able to communicate fully what he endured so we can treat him to his illness and not to his symptoms.

Without a medical examination, we are also excluding substance or general medical factors for Miles' symptoms (again, this could change with more observation or a review of Miles' medical records). The type of schizophrenia appears to be Paranoid. The delusions that Miles is suffering are prosecutory in nature and revolve around humiliation and possibly being socially ostracized due to small genital size, morbid obesity and some as yet unknown secret that Miles is carrying. This falls in line with the DSM criteria. It should also be noted that Miles appears to have a high level of functioning (he is able to perform logical deductions and function within society at some level) and individuals suffering from paranoid type schizophrenia do have a better prognosis in regard to functioning (APA, 2000).

There is not enough information present within this interview to assign a longitudinal course with any certainty, but the length of Miles' reported symptoms would lead me to believe that he would be classified as 'continuous.'

Axis II: Personality Disorders

Mental Retardation

Diagnostic Code DSM-IV Name

301.6 Dependent Personality Disorder (please see notes below)

Axis III: General Medical Conditions

ICD-9-CM Code ICD-9-CM Name

None

Axis IV: Psychosocial and Environmental Problems

X Problems related to the social environment. Due to Miles' delusions, his relationship with others is strained. The persecution and humiliation scenarios defy logic and Miles feels as if he is constantly under scrutiny. He is especially dangerous and violent whenever he perceives that someone is watching him eat.

X Educational problems as indicated in Rodney's interview.

Axis V: Global Assessment of Functioning Scale

Score: 30 "Behavior is considerably influenced by delusions or hallucinations" (APA, 2000). Time Frame: Current.

Miles feels that he is being mocked and ostracized for his physical deformity and other issues. His behavior is indicative of someone who is being persecuted and, therefore, the attitude of people around him will support that perception. Culturally, Miles is a Caucasian male that speaks English and one can only assume that his societal norms follow those most standard in the United States or Canada. His familial status is wealthy, so that is a boon in his favor. This means that his delusions can not be culturally attributed. The focus of genitalia size is derivative of the 'size matters' culture and media atmosphere in North America, so Miles' current fixation on that is reasonable. Even early in life, Miles reported that he felt 'different' from everybody else. Cruelty in locker rooms, especially in reference to physical attributes, is commonplace. It would be interesting to try and determine whether or not Miles' break manifested due to a series of stressors in that regard compounded by his island experiences. Only time will tell.

EPILOGUE

10 years later

"HOW MANY ARE left?" Miles asked, eyeing the gathering of people that extended out the door. The line resembled a never-ending centipede, coiling and wriggling around the various displays in the bookstore.

"It doesn't matter," his agent whispered, "you're only here for another hour. Some will go home disappointed, but if they want to meet you bad enough, they'll catch you at the next signing."

"I wish I'd never written this book," Miles said, putting on a fake smile as a portly woman approached him with her young son in tow.

The woman slapped the book down and Miles stared at it. *My Summer as a Cannibal* was displayed in red with the corners dripping down as if to simulate blood. It was pretty cheesy, and Miles had objected to it, and the title, the entire time, but once the contracts were signed he'd lost most of his rights to the book. Just sit back and enjoy the fat royalty checks, his agent had told him. Miles couldn't help but laugh. Royalty checks meant nothing if you were already wealthy.

"Can you make it out to Julia?" the woman asked, smacking her gum as she talked. The little boy seemed transfixed by Miles.

"Sure thing."

He flipped open the book and settled on the cover page. *For Jenny* caught his eye, and he felt the slightest sting of a tear start to form. It had been 10 years, and he still missed her every day. One of the only good things to come out of the book was that her memory was preserved and kept intact. She hadn't resorted to the barbarism that the rest of the camp succumbed to, and Miles felt good knowing her parents didn't have to live with the shame of their daughter turning into a psychopath.

He scribbled the signature and handed it to the woman. She thanked him, and yanked her son along. Miles glanced at the clock. There were still 58 minutes remaining. He sighed.

The next pair to arrive were two gangly looking teenagers, each clutching a book. Miles knew what was probably coming next, and they didn't disappoint.

"Dude, you fucking ate people? That's pretty gross," the skinnier one said, handing his book to Miles, who took it away with some force, hoping to show displeasure. The stockier kid chortled.

"Guys, let's keep it clean. My friend had to do some pretty awful things to stay alive. Read the book and see for yourself." His agent stepped up and glared at the young punks.

"Sorry, sorry. No disrespect, bro."

"I can't wait for the movie," the other one said.

"Movie?" Miles looked at the kid and then to his agent, who stared at the ground.

“Yeah, they just announced it on a forum I follow that Matt Damon and Ben Affleck have signed on to play you and Charles York, and apparently they are going to go with more of a dark comedy.”

Miles felt the urge to vomit rise in his throat. The entire ordeal he’d gone through was far from funny. He’d lost the first girl he’d ever loved, his sanity, and his childhood. The agent and Miles would have some words once the signing was done.

“Just move along, kids,” the agent instructed, and they did.

“What the fuck, Gene?” Miles whipped around, furious. The next person in line stopped in his tracks, watching the heated exchange.

“Look, we can talk about it later. The rights to the movie and book are separate, and I was going to tell you after the signing. We’ll have a meeting and discuss the creative license the director wants to take with the movie.”

“Yes, we will,” Miles said, and turned back to the next person. The clock showed 50 minutes remained.

Time ran as slow as Miles did.

***

“Honey? Kids? I’m home.” Miles walked through the palatial home.

His parents had bought the place for him when he’d been medically cleared to rejoin society from the psychiatrist. It was secluded and safe from gawkers and curious news agencies whose lust for the gory details never seemed to be sated. That was the entire reason why he’d written the book, though it had been a project he’d protested vehemently at first. His doctor encouraged him, saying it would be good therapy to get the whole story out. All it did was garner Miles more attention than he'd ever wanted. He wished to just blend back in with society, but that was becoming a dream he'd never realize.

"Hey sweetheart, how was the signing," his wife, Penelope, greeted him with a kiss and took his briefcase.

"About as disastrous as one could imagine. People just don't know how to filter themselves from saying rude stuff. And, get this, I found out they are making a movie out of the entire ordeal. A comedy, if you can believe it."

"Well, that's pretty insensitive. Honestly, this society is going to hell quicker than I could imagine."

She hugged him, and Miles took in the smell of lilac and vanilla. She was too good for him and whether she was with him for money or not, she hid it very well by being an excellent mother and wife. She was his physical therapist, and the two had fallen in love working together every day for long hours. Sessions morphed into coffee, which turned into dinner. Before he knew it, she was offering him a different kind of therapy. She'd read his book and discussed things with him. The craziest part was that she understood what he did and why. She never judged and each day he loved her more.

"The kids just finished their baths. Go sit in your favorite chair and I'll bring you a vodka and tonic."

"Twist of lime?"

"Of course." She kissed him. "Dinner will be ready soon. We are having one of your favorites, braised cheeks in gravy with rice."

"Now I'm happy," he said and walked to the living room and sat down to the massive big screen TV.

He turned it on, and was immediately greeted by

the smiling faces of Matt Damon and Ben Affleck. The words *Camp Yum Yum* were situated over their heads. He'd make sure to call his lawyer in the morning. Camp Yum Yum? Really? He turned the TV off.

Giggling laughter and fast feet on hardwood floor caused his ears to perk, and two balls of unconditional love plopped on his lap, covering him with hugs and kisses. He laughed and hugged them back. Becoming a father was the greatest thing to ever happen to him. They discussed their day at school, all things fascinating through the eyes of a child. A little boy and a girl, both in the spitting image of their parents. What more could a man want? Penelope handed him a drink, and his life was complete. Miles nodded off.

"Dinner is ready," Penelope's voice called from the kitchen, rousing Miles from his nap. He collected the children and the trio got up and moved into the dining room.

Miles helped get the kids settled before moving into the kitchen, where Penelope was using tongs to move something around in a large cast iron pot. He walked over and looked down at the succulent brown gravy. The chunk of meat turned, and a smiling, skeletal face stared at him. Judging by the smells, this would be Penelope's finest meal yet.

"Where'd you find him?"

"He got caught in one of our traps. I swear, we have a sign saying this is private property, yet hunters still insist in walking through our woods. It was kind of sad. He honestly thought I was coming to help him. Thanked me over and over again, until I slit his throat."

Miles let out a chuckle. "Where's the rest of him?"

"Already processed and in the freezer. It's been a busy day."

"Poor baby. I'll give you a foot rub tonight."

She kissed him and shooed him out the kitchen while she plated the food. Miles sat around the table and stared at his family shoveling heaps of meat and rice into their mouths. Laughter and good times filled the table, and, as Miles chewed on the human flesh, he couldn't help but think of himself as a teenager, sitting back in the dining hall of Camp Tum Tum.

GLAMGINA

David C. Hayes

AT FIRST, REGINALD Miller thought he was suffering from incredibly painful gas. The kind of painful, gurgling, gas bubbles that people think are heart attacks wracked his body. The pain centered in Reginald's lower abdomen and swayed, from lower to upper intestine, like some 1940s dirigible on a crash course with his testicles. Reginald had the feeling, though, that this could be special. He felt as if something wonderful was happening and, if it was what he thought it was, this special moment started many years ago . . . at the carnival.

Growing up gay in the 'enlightened' eighties wasn't really all it was cracked up to be. Reginald lived in a small Illinois town, with small Illinois friends and family. After watching an episode of *Punky Brewster* that filled Reginald with early-teenage confidence, he came out to both his parents and friends. The beatings started soon after and Reginald, bleeding and bruised, fled into the night with only the clothes he was wearing and his anxiety disorders as baggage.

After a few weeks on the road, Reginald stumbled upon his life's calling. The Fairhaven Brothers Traveling Carnival was in need of a strong young man to help with setting up and tearing down. All lifestyles accepted . . . no questions asked. As Reginald spoke with Mr. Harvey, the ring leader (for lack of a better term), and heir to the original Fairhaven Brothers, tears welled in the young man's eyes. Mr. Harvey, using all of his six foot frame and long white beard to look distinguished and credible, discussed how free and democratic the carnival was . . . where anyone of any race, creed, color, orientation or deformity are accepted as equals. Reginald broke down, just then, weeping in heaving gasps like waves crashing against the shore.

Mr. Harvey, having been in the carnival business for some time and well-versed in emotional breakdowns, knelt down and stroked Reginald's head. In the past couple of decades, Mr. Harvey had experienced so many coming of age success stories he had lost count.

"We're a family here, kid. All of us're freaks . . . that's just how it is," Mr. Harvey said as he stood. The young man looked up using his own shirt to dry the tears. Reginald stood as well, sniffling, and hugged Mr. Harvey. Mr. Harvey laughed, only slightly surprised, and returned the hug. The old carnival master led Reginald to the labor bunks and, for the first time in a long time, Reginald slept.

Over time Reginald proved himself to the carnies. He worked hard, from first light to last, and paid extremely close attention to anyone he perceived to be his elder (and that included almost everyone). He grew strong, tall and handsome (beautiful to some), and he possessed that strange magnetism that drew people to him that only the very good politicians, society-changing philanthropists and serial killers seem to have. Reginald learned about all of the carnival's operations from games to food to rides to shows and, in short order, was a veritable carnival encyclopedia. What really grabbed his attention, though, was the freak show. The Alligator Boy, the Bearded Lady and the rest fascinated Reginald and he spent as much time as he could with the freaks. Reginald felt as if he fit in . . . he was one of the crowd. Best of all Reginald felt as if he had found a home that came complete with a first-time lover.

The carnival, oddly, has the same statistical proportion of homosexuals as the rest of the United States. One in ten, or 10 percent, of the American population is believed to be homosexual. Out of the, roughly, one hundred carnival regulars, nine were gay. Reginald, of course, the Bearded Lady, of course, three laborers (who had found the carnival much in the same way Reginald did), two clowns, one of the trapeze artists and the star of the freak show, Miss Mann, the carnival's resident half man/half woman. Miss Mann, or Don, was in his mid-60s and really pushing the envelope of performance integrity. Reginald quickly became fascinated with Don's tranny show and Don, in turn, quickly became fascinated with Reginald's eighteen-year-old ass. Don showed Reginald the ins and outs of professional transvestite performance including how to work the crowd, when to display your 'manly' side, lip syncing and, most importantly, wardrobe design. In turn, Reginald gave Don unfettered access to his body, making Reginald malleable and permissive no matter how depraved Don's desires were. Reginald was groomed to take over Don's performances and he viewed the constant degradation as a small price to pay for the knowledge.

Truthfully, Reginald felt as if his worldview had expanded, thanks to Don. In that small Illinois town Reginald had no idea what a dildo was, much less how to take a fisting session. Don exposed Reginald to an entirely new world that, much to his own surprise, Reginald really did enjoy. Even though the rest of the carnival, especially his friends in the freak show, could tell that Reginald was changing . . . a little here, a little there, Reginald maintained he was the same as always if a bit more mature. He had become darker, more concerned with his hierarchal standing within the carnival, and envious of Don's headliner status.

Quickly, Reginald's prowess as a transvestite eclipsed Don's. Regina, as he now insisted everyone call him, was a natural. He owned the stage from the second the lights came up and could play the audience with the best of them. Regina lip-synched flawlessly, especially the Barbra Streisand songs, and walked the stage like a catwalk. Even the end-of-show denouement, as Regina revealed Reginald to the crowd, was spectacularly done. Don watched his young protégé work the afternoon shows, for less money, and knew then and there that he, that damn old queen, was obsolete. Unfortunately for Don, so did Regina.

Becoming Regina was like flipping a switch for Reginald. Regina worked the stage. Regina took control, even while having sex with Don or the gay clowns. Regina wouldn't have taken that shit back in Illinois . . . she was hardcore. Regina had fans as well. Slowly but surely, Reginald would recognize repeat customers in the audience. Smiling, leering, salivating, raging hard-ons . . . no matter how they manifested it, each of them had a jones for Regina and she decided it was time to get out of the afternoon slot and make a real name in the tranny business.

Don, literally, didn't see it coming. His face was buried in a pillow at the time and the level of his ecstasy was so complete, so perfect, that he barely noticed a little more pressure on the back of his head until it was far too late. Reginald finished, in both senses, stood back from Don's corpse and smiled. A few crocodile tears as he lamented the accidental erotic asphyxiation death of this lover and Regina would take the main stage in whatever town they happened to be in that week.

A few more months headlining and Regina hit on her best idea yet. The salivating, pecker-pulsing fans that came to see her perform the same old songs again and again could be separated from even more of their money. Reginald had changed. Regina made most of the decisions and Regina decided that those local yokels, from town to town, would pay big money to throw a hump in her ass. They would lose their minds, rubbing their dicks through the overalls as she performed and spending all that farm subsidy money on seeing Regina perform again and again. Regina considered it a business decision with a solid plan and a built-in clientele. The clowns would get a little jealous, but fuck 'em. The little piece of Reginald, crammed deep down inside and hidden behind a sequined curtain in Regina's mind, balked at the thought of becoming a prostitute but realized quickly (more out of self preservation than logic) that spreading those legs for the fans just may be a nice 'thank you' and a way to give back. At least the little piece of Reginald would repeat that, over and over again, as sweaty farmers, married tycoons and any manner of depraved rabble corn-holed Regina night after night. The money piled up as the carnival moved its way across the Bible Belt.

Mr. Harvey was aware of the moonlighting and was as displeased as could be. He remembered the day Reginald came to the carnival and cursed himself for letting Don get his hooks in the young man. Mr. Harvey also faced another quandary. It was common knowledge, within the small carnie family, that Reginald pretty much 'took' the top spot in the show and Harvey wanted nothing more than to keep the normal world out of his carnival. Lost in thought, Mr. Harvey didn't notice the tent flap open and, like a b-movie coincidence, one of the gay clowns burst through in a flutter.

"Mr. Harvey! Come quick . . . Regina just blacked out on stage!"

Harvey leapt to his feet and hurried from his tent. No matter what he or anyone else thought Reginald had done, the boy was still a part of this family and when he needed help, Harvey would be there.

As Harvey entered the performance tent the Alligator Boy and Bearded Lady were already refunding money to the patrons. Good, that would keep them out of his hair. He scanned the area and saw Reginald crumpled on the floor, dark blood pooling around the young man and clashing wildly with his orange and green costume. He was doubled over in pain. Like a collection of ghoulish mannequins, the rest of the performers stood in a ring around the poor lad and Harvey couldn't understand why no one would get closer to help. Mr. Harvey stepped forward and was nearly felled by a wall-like stench radiating from Reginald. Pulling his flannel over his nose, Mr Harvey moved in toward Reginald. He had mistakenly thought that Reginald was lying in a pool of dark, oxygenated-blood which, Harvey learned much to his chagrin, was truly a fetid puddle of excrement leaking uncontrollably outward on the stage. With each inch gained by the puddle, Reginald's fellow onlookers took a step back. Harvey, using all the will made available to him and attempting to channel the love he has for every carnie into a single act, scooped Reginald from the floor and carried him, toward the door of the tent. Trailing behind them, quite a bit behind them, the remaining carnies marched along like a funeral procession avoiding the small splotches of Reginald left behind that punctuated Harvey's steps.

Harvey knew, as did everyone else, that this was serious and Reginald needed immediate medical attention. Without missing a beat, and damning the thought of reaching out to a bunch of normals outside the carnival for help, Harvey laid Reginald out in the bed of his pick up truck on a garbage bag and prepared for the ride into town.

The local medical center was open and Reginald was admitted. Mr. Harvey sat in the waiting room for what seemed like hours. A doctor, sweaty and exhausted, walked up to Mr. Harvey who was mid-way through his tenth cup of burnt hospital coffee.

"Mr. Harvey?" the doctor asked.

Harvey stood, "Yes."

The doctor avoided Mr. Harvey's gaze and spun. The doctor motioned and walked quickly toward the hospital room. "Follow me."

Without a word, Mr. Harvey followed the doctor.

The doctor and Mr. Harvey entered the small,

dimly lit hospital room. In a fetal position, with his back toward the door, Reginald slept peacefully. He wore a hospital gown, carefully covering only the most essential body areas.

"Will he be all right?" Mr. Harvey asked.

The doctor took a deep breath and shook his head.

"I have to tell you something. Reginald has given me permission since you are to be his primary caretaker," the doctor began and Mr. Harvey nodded.

"I understand."

"Not really." The doctor reached down and flipped Reginald's hospital gown over exposing his buttocks.

What Mr. Harvey saw chilled him to his bones. He knew that what he was looking at should have resembled a young man's rear end. What Mr. Harvey was looking at, though, resembled the mouth of a homeless man after someone had punched all of the teeth away. Massive scar tissue lumped around itself and any structural integrity seemed lost. Reginald's anus resembled a glazed donut with a tractor tread running through it.

The doctor flipped Reginald's gown back as Mr. Harvey wretched. Bent over, sucking in air, Mr. Harvey attempted to compose himself.

"I understand that this can be, well, shocking."

Mr. Harvey looked up, wiping spittle away from his lips, "How, what . . . dear God!"

"This, Mr. Harvey, is the result of severe and repeated trauma. After an interview with Reginald, we assume he has been engaging in anal intercourse with multiple partners every evening for approximately one and one half years. All musculature on his anus has broken down. The cosmetic damage is simply the visual manifestation of how the final phase of Reginald's digestive system works now. His sphincter is effectively destroyed. He's . . . he's a . . . "

"A dripper?" Mr. Harvey tried to help.

"For lack of a better term, sure. We had to act quickly and in order to give Reginald the best chance at a normal life we opted to perform surgery and have given Reginald a colostomy."

Mr. Harvey's eyes grew wide. This is exactly why he avoided the normals. They could have probably fixed Reginald at the carnival with some tent stakes and elephant ears.

"We have rerouted Reginald's intestines and created a permanent stoma on his abdomen wall. This will now function as Reginald's rectal pore, for lack of a better term. All waste material will need to be routed to a small pouch that we will affix.

We have sutured the . . . area . . . of the damage shut. I have to warn you, there can be no more damage done to Reginald's, uuh, private area. He has already impacted his life to a great degree here."

"Understood, doctor. Will this affect his career as a . . . stage performer?"

"With Reginald's lack of insurance, we only felt comfortable using older materials and, unfortunately, he could possibly spring a leak at any moment. In addition, the mylar bag is large and bulky and will resemble a large cyst even under loose clothing."

"You can't do anything else?"

"Not with the money you people make. I'm very sorry."

Mr. Harvey hung his head, knowing the truth when he heard it.

The doctor nodded and, breathing deeply, exited

the room. Mr. Harvey turned his gaze on the sleeping Reginald. He took a seat next to the boy resisting the temptation to flip the hospital gown up again and take another look . . . it was like a car accident.

"You're a damn fool, kid . . . a damn fool."

Mr. Harvey stroked Reginald's hair and waited for the young man to wake up so he could give him the news of his new anus.

The return to the carnival was not a cause for celebration. As Reginald recovered, the freak show was headlined by the Alligator Boy and, by all accounts, he was doing an admirable job. Reginald's job duties were transferred to the ticket booth where he could disappear for 'leakage' issues and it would not impact the carnival-going experience for the customer.

Reginald quickly slipped into a funk. A major depressive order. He could no longer perform. He could no longer 'entertain' his gentleman visitors after the shows and, worst of all, he was broke. His entire life savings went to the damned colostomy and ticket taker wages were a fraction of what a headliner would make. Reginald tried to be mad at Mr. Harvey, but realized that he owed the man his life.

A few times a day, Reginald would need to remove the bulky bag, empty it and swab the opening. The first few times made his stomach churn but he quickly became accustomed to the practice. It was during a mid-day evacuation of his bowels into the bag when Regina stepped out of the darkness and hit on her greatest idea ever. Reginald felt himself slipping behind that sequined curtain again and, truth be told, he liked the nothingness . . . missed it. Regina, though, was chomping at the bit and had big plans.

She finished cleaning the ostomy and stoma, replaced the bag and headed for the clown tent.

The gay clowns, feeling sorry for Reginald, tended to dote on the young man. Regina entered their tent to truly happy greetings and asked for a few simple things that Mr. Harvey had requested. She left with various tubes of make-up and glitter spray. Upon returning to her tent, Regina began the arduous task of contacting her very large client list. She promised them an entirely new experience, something that only Regina could provide and that no price would be too great. The next town the carnival entered would see the re-debut of Regina!

That next town, the following week, played host to the carnival as usual. After the freak show ended, per Regina's instructions, the first of her new clientele lined up in the dark just outside her tent. Regina had told them that discretion was the key to the entire operation and that they would not be disappointed.

Regina's tent was darkened with only a solitary red glow emanating from within. Tyrone Lewis, soybean farmer and registered sex offender, stomped his feet in anticipation. He was first in line and, thinking of how incredible Regina was before, could only imagine what delights lay within the tent. He reflexively wiped his hands off on his dirty overalls waiting for . . .

"Come in, please," Regina's husky, sultry voice beckoned.

Tyrone nearly jumped out of his skin and smiling to the remaining men in line, ducked inside the tent.

"Well, Tyrone . . . I thought you'd be first," Regina moaned. She was lying on her divan, dressed in her former performance costume as gorgeous as ever. Her limbs lay akimbo in, beckoning any suitor that came her way.

"Yes, Ma'am, wouldn't miss it fer the world! Heard your, your . . . privates were messed up and that made me real sad."

Regina chuckled, "Guess you just can't keep a good girl down . . . let's see what you brought me, Tyrone."

Nearly giggling in happiness, Tyrone stripped out of the overalls. A big ape, he stood in the red light, breathing heavily. His erection bobbed with each breath.

"How we gonna do it?"

Regina slowly rolled up her costume as she turned on her side.

"Like you've never done it before, behold . . . " Regina finished rolling her costume up to reveal the colostomy. The bag had been removed and the opening had been decorated in make-up and glitter resembling a pair of lips, " . . . the Glamgina!" Regina's replacement anus glowed in the red light and seemed to pulse with an energy of its own making. The moment was magical.

Tyrone sucked in a breath as the reality of the situation hit his pea brain.

"It's . . . it's . . . " he stammered.

Regina bit her lip, waiting on his reaction. This gamble could end up going poorly in a very violent way.

"Glorious," Tyrone managed to squeak out. He shakily moved forward, approaching the Glamgina. Regina threw her head back like a 1950s starlet.

"Take me!" Regina said and, if she didn't know better, she felt as if the Glamgina smiled as Tyrone descended upon it.

Regina managed to keep this particular little secret from the rest of the carnival for many, many months. Town after town, man after man, deposit after deposit, the Glamgina entertained one and all. Regina's finances improved drastically and she found that she could charge a great deal more for this particular service. New customers, hearing of Regina's gift, would flock to the little carnival tent after the amusements had closed to have an experience unlike any other. After all, where else on the planet could one find a willing Glamgina?

The abdominal pain started a few days ago and Regina just knew that something important was happening. She had cancelled her appointments for the rest of the week and was contemplating retirement entirely. After a few quick calculations she estimated that the Glamgina had entertained over a thousand happy customers, night after night. She knew, then and there, that the magic of the Glamgina, the happiness and joy that the Glamgina represented, could not be contained. The abdominal pain surged again and, this time, she could feel it grow inside her. Actual . . . feel . . . it. Regina lay on her back and closed her eyes. As happy as she was, Reginald would make a better mother. Massaging the Glamgina, Regina/Reginald fell asleep to dream of family picnics, blind love and how fortunate they were to be at the carnival where no questions were ever asked.

THE CHEST

Mark C. Scioneaux

THE NIGHT WAS dark and cold, but Frannie Mae didn't care one bit. Stumbling in the darkness, letting only the pale light of the full moon illuminate her path, she made her way to the Peaceful Rest cemetery. There was someone resting there who was about to get a piece of her mind.

Her head swirled with liquor, and her mouth bobbed open as she tromped her muddy boots through fallen branches and pools of dank water. It had rained the night before, and the uneven terrain was slick and choked with decaying leaves and other matter. Her right hand still clutched the empty bottle of whisky, and she wielded it in front of her in the night air as if attempting to smash the faces of invisible demons that taunted and jabbed her with tiny pitchforks.

She threw open the rusted iron gates; her ears ringing as the metal screeched for oil. Shambling through the rows of marked graves, she fell down on her knees at the one with fresh dirt mounded on top. Fat tears washed down her cheeks, creating streaks down her dirt-caked face.

"William Joseph Ramsey." She read the words etched in stone aloud, and then slammed her empty bottle into the marker, causing it to shatter into innumerable shards.

"You tell me where that money is, you old bastard! Billie Joe, I know you can hear me in there. You owe me that money."

She paused as if expecting a response. The only sound was the fall wind whipping through dead branches, blowing off the last remaining leaves that clung to their mother before falling and rotting on the ground with the rest of their wayward brethren. An owl hooted in the distance and a dog sounded its mournful wail.

"I don't have any more money. You didn't leave me nothing in the will but the damn house, and it ain't worth shit, and you knew that. Just tell me where you left the savings. You bury it somewhere? I done checked the barn, the house, the closets. Everywhere!"

Still, she received no answer. Her breath came out in ghostly vapors and her heart thumped rapidly.

"I hope you rot in there forever. I hope there ain't no heaven for a mean, cruel miser like yourself. You know, I actually felt bad about pushing you down those stairs. But now, if I could do it all over again I would. I swear to the Lord above I would! And spit on your damn corpse!"

She collapsed onto the grave, her fingers digging into soft dirt and her tears made tiny mud puddles on the fresh soil. She sobbed until her throat was too raw to continue, and all moisture had left her body.

"In . . . the chest . . . "

Frannie jumped up, her face stark white and

confused, convinced that her mind was playing tricks. Whipping her head around, she looked for someone, a practical joker perhaps, who followed her out and was playing games. She was alone, and that realization iced her blood.

"Just the booze talking," she said, laughing at the thought of her dead husband communicating with her from beyond. "It's only the booze. I swear I ain't drinking another drop."

"The chest . . . Frannie Mae . . . "

The voice said, louder this time and as hollow and empty as a newly dug grave. Frannie Mae lurched to her feet and ran, screaming like the devil himself was hot on her tail. She didn't stop until she reached the safety of her home, latched the door, and drained dry the only other bottle of whiskey she had in the house.

***

Frannie Mae sat on her front porch, rocking back and forth in the old wooden chair her late husband had made when a pickup truck stopped in front, kicking up a kiss of gravel and dirt. She pressed a cold compress to her head, helping ease away the terrible headache from the night before. She'd overdone it. Drank so damn much that she was hearing things. A little hair of the dog would ease her back down to Earth, and she took another sip of the ketchup and vodka concoction she'd dubbed a poor woman's Bloody Mary. She saw the truck coming down the road, but paid it no mind. Even when it pulled in front of her house and stopped, she still didn't care.

Long legs clothed in a pair of faded blue jeans swung out the cab, and two brown boots touched the ground. The young man looked up at the house, and then at the farm. He adjusted the blue flannel shirt he had tucked into his pants and ran a hand over his brown hair, pushing it aside. He closed the door and walked around the truck, stopping at the stairs leading up to the porch.

"Aunt Frannie, it's me, Jason."

Frannie lifted the compress up and stared down at the well dressed and handsome young man. She hadn't seen one of her sister's kids in ages. Not since she and Arlene had a huge fight over the way Billie Joe had treated Frannie.

"Jason, it's been so long. What made you drive all this way to come see me?"

She sat up in the rocking chair and attempted to stand. Her head sloshed like an overturned bottle, and she fell back in the chair. Jason ran up the steps and helped his aunt to her feet. They exchanged a long hug, and she patted his face, feeling it to make sure he was really there and not just some apparition. Her sister had three kids, and Jason had always been her favorite.

"I heard about Uncle Bill. I wanted to come and pay my respects, is all. I'm sorry we didn't come to the funeral, but I was out of town at school and well, you know how it is between you and mom."

"Oh, I know, Jason. It's all right and I appreciate you coming by to see me. No one does anymore and it just warms my heart. How about you come in and I'll make us something to eat. I haven't eaten yet today."

He opened the door for her and they entered the house and walked into the kitchen. Frannie Mae opened the refrigerator but was embarrassed to see no food inside. She tried a cabinet, and it was empty as well. Jason stood by the entrance in silence, aware of what was transpiring. The woman buried her face in her hands and weeped. He walked over and placed a comforting hand on her shoulders.

"I ain't got nothing, Jason. When your uncle died he gave away all our money to the church and they won't give me a dime even though they know I'm starving."

"But I thought Uncle Bill had plenty of money. He was always giving us dollars when we came over. He has to have something hidden around the house."

"I know he has a great deal of it somewhere. I don't know why, but for some reason I think it may be in a chest somewhere. But I've done checked this house a hundred times over and I can't find nothing."

"Look, I'm here now and I can help you, but you need to eat something. Let me drive down to the store and buy you some food. That way you can cook for us and we can talk about where to look."

"Oh, you sweet boy. I couldn't ask you to do that."

"I won't have any of that. At least let me do it as a way of saying sorry that I couldn't make the funeral."

She relented and Jason strolled out the house and drove off toward the only store in the small town. An hour passed and he returned, his arms bulging with paper bags filled to the brim with eggs, milk, bread, and all kinds of good things to eat. Frannie Mae started on bacon and eggs while Jason got a pot of coffee going and put some biscuits in the oven.

They sat at the table and ate in silence; the only sounds the clang of silverware and the smacking of lips. Jason sipped his coffee and Frannie Mae sopped up runny yolk with a hot biscuit.

"So, I'll make you a deal, Jason. You help me find that money and I'll give you some of it. No sense in me keeping it all for myself if you find it."

"Sure, Aunt Frannie. Sounds good to me. Being in school I could use all the money I can get."

"Don't your parents help you out?"

"Yeah, they do. But it still cost a lot to go out, and you know, meet girls." He smiled sheepishly and looked down.

"Well I hope you meet a nice one and bring her to meet your Aunt Frannie one day."

They spent the rest of the day talking about where to look and areas Frannie Mae had already searched. The barn would be the easiest since the building was empty and open. The house, on the other hand, was another story. Too many nooks and crevices made any spot the perfect place to stash some money.

Night came and Frannie Mae made up the guest room for Jason. He thanked her, and she was happy to have another person to share the house with, even temporarily. She entered her room and got into bed, bringing the covers up close to her neck. The night rolled on but she remained awake, unable to sleep. Every time she closed her eyes, Frannie heard that dead voice calling from the grave. Billie Joe's dead voice.

***

"You look like you didn't sleep a wink, Aunt Frannie," Jason said as he sipped his coffee.

She felt terrible, and probably looked worse, but she was bound and determined to find that money today and stop all the worrying.

They had breakfast, and started their search in the barn. Like she'd thought, it yielded nothing. Jason checked the ground diligently for any shovel marks or overturned dirt. He found nothing. He walked around the perimeter, trying to locate a loose board or pocket, but, again, his search was fruitless.

With the barn cleared, they turned to the house, attacking each room one at a time and leaving nothing unturned. Jason found a twenty dollar bill wadded up between a couch cushion, and Frannie Mae snatched a five dollar bill from behind the entertainment center. She'd been certain she'd looked, but knew her old eyes weren't as sharp as they'd once been. Still, they'd searched the entire day and only came up with $25 in wayward money that anyone could have stumbled upon.

Night fell and the two treasure hunters sat at the table, eating a meatloaf Frannie Mae had prepared. She almost screamed when Jason smacked the table and shot up.

"Jason, what? You nearly scared the life out of me!"

"What about the attic? Have you checked it?"

"The attic? Your Uncle Bill was a sick man. He couldn't have made it to the attic and I'm in no shape to go up there, either. So, no, I haven't been up there in years."

"Then that's where we'll look. It's the only place left we haven't tried."

"Finish your dinner. We can go up there in the morning."

"I can't. I'm too excited. Let's go now. Besides, if that money is in there, we might be eating steak tonight!"

She handed him a flashlight, explaining the light had burnt out up there some time ago and neither she or Billie Joe could change it. They walked up the stairs to the second floor. The pair reached the door to the attic at the end of the hall quickly, a little breathless. Jason turned the knob and Frannie Mae clutched his shirt as they climbed up the narrow stairwell to the attic above.

The air was dusty and hot. Jason guided Frannie Mae over the air conditioner coils and to the large mounds of various items that had been stored in the attic and forgotten about. Frannie Mae stood with the flashlight and aimed it where Jason asked her to as he opened boxes and rummaged through what they'd hoped would be the final chest.

There was one box left, a large wooden trunk, and Jason slid it into the open.

"It can't be that one, dear. That one has my wedding dress in it and, looking at the dust, it ain't been touched since the day it was put up here."

"Well, only one way to find out."

Jason opened the chest and, sure enough, a faded off-white dress was revealed.

"Dammit," he said, and grabbed the garment. The crunch of paper underneath the dress caused them both to gasp.

Removing the dress, his eyes widened at the two sacks underneath the gown. He opened one, and was amazed at the sight of hundreds of dollars in crisp bundled bills. They'd found the chest.

"You did it, Jason! You found the money."

Jason whipped his head around and smiled.

"Oh, I did find the money. *My* money!"

Frannie Mae's face dropped and her once frantic hands now hung lifeless at her sides. She couldn't believe the words coming out of the mouth of the only relative she'd ever actually liked.

"I . . . I don't understand." Tears welled in her tired eyes.

"Mom told me you called her for help and she let

it out that Uncle Bill stashed a pile of cash in the house. I just had to make the time to come find it, and that I did." He paused and flashed a wicked grin. "I don't give a shit about you. You or that sorry excuse for an uncle. Mom was right about not talking to the both of you. Now I'm going to take *my* money and go back to school. The next time you see me, I'll be staring down at your funeral."

He grabbed the two bags out the chest and shrugged past Frannie Mae, who stood motionless. He'd just passed her when a soft voice called.

"Jason . . . dear."

"Look, I don't have nothing to say—"

A shot from an old baseball bat knocked his teeth out.

He fell back, his head striking the floor and almost causing him to lose consciousness on the spot. The bags of money hit the ground and fell to the side, the stacks of bills spilling out. Streams of thick blood exploded in the air as he choked. His eyes were wide and scared. Frannie Mae stood over him, smiling. Her hands gripped the bat like a major league slugger.

"Looks like you found my money," she said, and raised the bat.

She brought it down hard, cracking her nephew's skull. His arms flopped to the side and she beat him over the head until they stopped moving. Laughing, she knelt down next to the fresh corpse and started to rummage through the money. She began to count and then suddenly stopped as the sound of footsteps boomed behind her.

The air changed. What was once hot and dry became instantly cool and dank. The sounds of nature eased and the only audible noise was the heavy breathing of something behind her. She whipped around, swinging the bannister wildly, but the intruder caught it and yanked her closer.

She stared into the rotting face of Billie Joe Ramsey.

She wanted to scream, but found her voice gone. His nose had rotted away and his teeth were bare from the skin that had pulled back over time. His cloudy eyes stared at her, accusing and filled with hate.

A tattered hand swiped the air, connecting with Frannie's face and dropping her to the ground where she crumpled into a ball out of shock and pure terror.

"*The chest . . .* " the thing said, as it picked up Frannie Mae and placed her inside. "*Final . . . rest.*"

It latched the chest and pushed it back into the shadows. Pausing over Jason, it shook its head and stumbled back to the graveyard, taking the money to rest with him eternally.

***

Frannie Mae opened her eyes and thought she'd gone blind. Her hands reached out, and she screamed as she touched the inside of the chest. Her wedding dress was on top of her, and she struggled to get it off her face as she clawed violently until her nails snapped and her fingers bled. Her husband had returned to claim the money that belonged to him, and to make sure a murderer was punished, never to be found again.

She screamed and cried for help, bleating for any kind of aid. For Jason. For someone to find her and rescue her. She screamed until she could scream no more.

THAT OTHER PLAN FROM OUTER SPACE

David C. Hayes

THE PABST BLUE Ribbon cans, nearly a case of them, rattled out of the cab of the truck when Randy opened the door to his 1982 F-150. The hinges creaked, giving the empty cans a little rhythm section to play off of. He chuckled and then lurched out of the truck himself. It was a good day. He got a job. Well, kind of a good day. Ever since the insurance company determined that Randy was goldbricking, faking an injury, and exploiting the workman's comp and disability pay, they had kicked him to the curb like some kind of criminal.

He wasn't a criminal, though. He had a legitimate injury and figured that a big company like McDonalds could afford to pay for a little bed rest. It just got too easy. Days of playing Madden led into weeks of playing Madden, drinking Pabst and looking at BBW porn on the internet. He got sucked into the lifestyle and maintained that pain from his back injury wouldn't allow him to work. The state, and the insurance company, kept him in rent/Pabst money and, as far as he was concerned, this was fine living indeed.

It was the goddamn heat lamp for the burgers that started the whole mess. Somehow, one of those idiot kids (Randy was 38) that worked with him must have bumped into the lamp. The lamp shifted and pointed directly at a patch of congealed grease on the floor. The heat from the lamp softened the grease and, boom, Randy went ass over heels and hit the floor hard. He was out cold, had a mild concussion and slipped a disc. A full thirty-six months later he was still on disability when he made a tragic mistake.

Randy liked the big girls. Always had. That was one of the reasons that he worked at Mickey D's (that and blowing off his entire senior year of high school and not seeing any merit in a GED since he wasn't going to be a college boy anyway because college boys were sissies and everyone knows that sissies get their asses kicked all the time . . . but that is a different story). The BBW, big beautiful women, frequented the restaurant regularly and Randy got his fill of eye candy. Big, overstuffed bags of eye candy. Like five pounds of candy in a sack that holds three. He was loving it. Better yet, Randy never spent a dime on food, eating the end of shift morsels meant for the garbage bin. If he did say so himself, he was living the sweet life. Until the accident and the Xbox addiction. Not being at the arches meant he didn't get to see what he called his "bubble babies," though, and that was a bit rough for him.

Randy reached into the cab of the truck and pulled out one of the last full Pabsts. He cracked it open and toasted the sky. Randy took a swig and then pulled the little piece of paper out of his pocket that served as the directions to his new job. He was sure that he followed them explicitly, but, as he gazed around the area, it didn't look like anything more than an abandoned field next to a broken down barn. And, for that matter, what kind of construction job started at 9pm? Randy shrugged and sloshed a little more of that hoppy goodness down his throat. He didn't care. If the job started that late, they should expect him to be a little lubed up.

He held the piece of paper up in the moonlight to read it. Luckily for him, none of the words had more than three syllables so he could sound it out pretty good.

"Root 33. Corn feel-d. Lite Con-struc-shon. 9 pm," he said. Nodding, Randy stuffed the paper back in his pocket and waited. Even though he missed his Madden, he smiled. The light of his life appeared one day, right out of the blue, and she was the reason he was even working right now. She was also the reason he got busted.

Even though he wasn't working, Randy still had enough friends that he could get a free meal or two at the arches whenever he needed one. This was most of the time. During one of his last visits, he managed to catch the eye of one of the largest, and loveliest, ladies he had ever seen. Her pouty lips were wrapped around a Big Mac and, if he weren't wearing a back brace (constructed out of an old weightlifting belt and orange suspenders he found at the Salvation Army) he would have slid up to that mama and swept her off her feet. He could only stare as special sauce dripped from the corner of her mouth and she expertly caught it with a plump index finger before it hit the ground, wasted.

Randy grinned, hard and wide, and, much to his amazement, that grin was returned. Not even the poppy seeds in her teeth could turn Randy away. He had to get to know her! Randy shambled, dragging one leg (he assumed that is how injured people walked), up to the young woman. He flattened his mullet down in the back and hitched his pants up as he moved, desperate to make a good first impression. The closer he got, the more beautiful she became.

Her hair was raven black and curled around her plump face. Her alabaster skin was perfect with no discernable joints to mar the curves. Her eyes were gold, truly, gold; the rose red of her cheeks the perfect shade of strawberry-kissed red. Large breasts draped over a larger belly and nothing was left to the imagination. She sported a Whitesnake t-shirt from the 1989 tour, three sizes too small, and poured herself into a pair of Daisy Dukes that morning just for Randy's benefit, he thought.

Randy's rebel flag was already at half-mast when he shuffled up to the table just in time to see the voluptuous vixen shove the last of her Big Mac into her mouth using a Chicken McNugget. Randy nearly lost it, right then and right there.

"Hey," he said, trying to sound smooth as silk, even with the back brace on, "my name's Randy, what's yours?"

She smiled and shoved another lump of processed chicken into her mouth.

"I get it, baby, I get it. Taking it slow. Can I buy you an apple pie?"

She raised an eyebrow, followed by another nugget.

Randy chuckled, "Oh, don't worry about me, I got

cash! I'm on disability . . . " He licked his lips, letting disability roll right off. He needed her to know that he was top of the food chain. Steady income, no bullshit.

She smiled and nodded. From that point forward, it seemed like they were inseparable.

Randy wasn't concerned when he did all the talking, he actually liked to hear himself. He didn't care that, aside from a few grunts and groans, Elsie (that was her name) only communicated via a notepad in short, simple sentences. Randy actually liked that. She was perfect for him: quiet, devoted and a beast in the sack.

The sex was great, from what Randy could remember. Every time he got a head of steam going, Elsie would drop down, south of the border, and stuff just went crazy. After a minute or two, his eyes would roll into the back of his head and he'd wake up an hour later feeling like a dried leaf. Wow.

They went everywhere together and it was in trying to impress Elsie that he got booted off of the disability rolls. Randy knew a guy that owned a mini golf outfit on Route 8 and both of them were proponents of the barter system. Randy slid the owner of "Nutter Putter" a Filet-O-Fish once a day for about a month, under the table, and Randy could come and go, playing putt putt, as much as he desired. He took Elsie there and, in the middle of showing off (making a particular difficult bank shot through a cardboard hockey goalie, up over a hill, and down a waterfall for a hole in one) he didn't notice his former manager from the restaurant playing two holes back. Davey Anderson, the twenty-something snot-nosed punk general manager of McDonald's #453 from Creek Craw, Michigan, had suspected that Randy was faking and, after a quick video taken from his iPhone, he could prove it.

'Nuff said. Randy was on the street, McDonalds and the insurance company decided not to press charges and, just like that, he was broke. Elsie swooped in to save the day.

Using her little notebook, and wrapping those exquisitely chubby fingers around a pen, she wrote the directions that Randy squinted to read in the moonlight moments ago. She assured him, in her own special 'down south' way, that she had his best interests at heart and that was enough for Randy.

Randy looked around the empty field, made out the husk of a burnt out barn in the growing gloom, and drained the last of his next to last can of Pabst. He thought that this may turn into a long evening when the sky erupted in light.

Brighter than anything he had ever seen before, an intense white light washed over Randy and the immediate area. He fell to the ground, arm over his eyes trying to keep his retinas from burning out, and cowered. A noise, like being behind a fighter jet taking off, blasted the immediate area followed by . . . something. It was brutal and strong, but Randy couldn't call it wind. It was just a force. A force that flattened him out on the ground, arms and legs splayed out as if he were about to make dirt angels. He couldn't make a sound, either. Even if he had something to say.

Although the force pinned him to the ground, paralyzing him, he had no trouble breathing. The intense light beamed onto him from something that hovered above was warm and it felt to Randy like the light was looking *inside* his body. He imagined an xray would feel like this, if it felt like anything. The noise blanketed the immediate area and Randy couldn't even hear himself think.

Then, Randy's body was lifted off of the ground. He tried to move his head from side to side, to no avail, and could only manage to strain his eyeballs as far right and as far left as possible to get some kind of gauge in regard to where he was going. As far as Randy could tell, he was going straight up, into the light. His peripheral vision caught a glimpse of some trees, telling him he was at least twenty feet high at that point. Then, the landmarks stopped and it was all sky and stars and moon.

And dark. The light winked out as Randy entered darkness. It looked like an inky black spot in the middle of the sky, like someone had just erased part of the stars. Randy, still immobile, slipped in there. Tears welled in the corners of his eyes and he thought of poor Elsie. What would she do without him?

***

Elsie stepped out of the wooded shadows and watched as Randy slipped into the floating Ink Pod. She smiled. Randy must have passed the initial scan or the Pod would never have accepted him. He'll be nice and cozy for his trip into orbit and the rendezvous with the Colony.

Elsie blinked twice and stood, hands akimbo, staring straight forward after Randy left. If anyone had been around, they could have sworn she was frozen there, in place. Nothing twitched, nothing moved. After a few more moments, Elsie hissed. Not like a snake, or a sparkly vampire, but as if the pneumatic brakes on a school bus had just been released. And then she split in half.

The two sides of Elsie split, right down the middle, and shuttered back like metallic theatre curtains to reveal two small, green men. If they were human, which they were not, they would have looked incredibly old. Septuagenarians at the very least, but tiny (no more than twelve to fourteen inches tall) and green. Within Elsie, the two little men sat in two little captain's chairs, one on top of the other in separate compartments. Each of them had a joystick-like controller rising up between their legs that looked to be how they controlled Elsie from the inside out.

Both of them sucked in a lungful of fresh, non-Elsie air, and exhaled loudly. A perfunctory high-five followed. The man on the bottom stretched his arms and yawned while the man on top pulled a headset microphone out from the arm of the chair and sat it on his head. The little man on the bottom spoke first in a voice that belonged on a Disney rodent.

"I never thought we'd get him out here . . . this guy was tough!"

"What are you talking about," the man on top answered, "you didn't have to deal with, what did he call it?"

"Sexy time."

"Yeah," the man on top nearly spat out. He shivered from the memory.

"You calling him in? After this one, we should get a bonus."

"Definitely. This BBW Model 9000 Abductee Attraction Unit is the best idea you've ever had! Slim pickings there for quite some time. If we didn't get a subject soon, I'm not sure the mother ship would have renewed our contract."

"Tell me about it. We haven't had any good test

subjects since the humans invented basic cable channels. Even the . . . crap. I always forget what they call them . . . ”

“Rednecks? Hillbillies?” The man on top offered.

“Yeah! Even they were getting wise. Can’t break the cardinal rule!”

“Only abduct humans that have no credibility. Recruitment 101!”

Both the man on top and the man on bottom laughed. Then, realizing their work wasn’t completely done, they sighed.

“Call it in,” the man on the bottom said.

“On it,” the man on the top returned.

“Oh, and make sure they set the anal probe to stun.”

“Isn’t it always?”

AN UNEXPECTED HUNT

Mark C. Scioneaux

"YOU SEE IT?"

"Do you see me raising my gun? You think I saw it?" Paul asked. He brought the Thermos to his mouth and took a sip of black coffee.

Mark shook his head and laid his rifle to the side. Space was limited inside the deer stand. The two large men nearly sat in one another's laps. They wouldn't move, though. No matter how cold the weather turned or how intense the frosty Tennessee air was as it whipped from the mountains; they'd come for one thing only: the golden stag.

"You sure this thing's even real?" Mark asked. He removed a cigarette from a pack and placed it in his mouth.

"Yes, I'm sure. And so are you. You heard the stories. Remember?" Paul crushed the cig before Mark struck his lighter. "And smoke'll scare any animal off. Use your brain."

"Sorry."

Tales of the golden stag had consumed the small town of Cedar Bend. It was a deer. Not just any old mangy deer, but a magnificent specimen with a brilliant coat and a crown of antlers so glorious people claimed they were carved by God himself. And the glow. The ones who'd seen it couldn't quite explain it, but the deer gave off an ethereal light that shimmered around its chestnut brown pelt.

It stood to reason that hunters wanted to add the unique prize to their trophy collection.

Paul viewed the deer as his meal ticket. If he could make this kill, he just knew it'd give him the opportunity to star in his own reality show. *Appalachian Adventurers* is what he'd call it. That is if his careless oaf of a cousin wouldn't scare the thing off before it stepped into his crosshairs.

"We been at this all day and all night." Mark adjusted his rear, shifting his weight. "My stomach's rumbling and I'm getting tired. Besides, ain't we supposed to be hunting deer? What good is us sitting in a tree staring at a plot of feeder corn?"

"Deer eat the corn. We shoot the deer." Paul felt annoyed, but humored his poor cousin. "Besides, with as many people I know going after this thing, you don't want to walk through the woods and have one of them idiots from the bar put a bolt in you. Talk about ruining your day. And then *I* got to tell grandma why you ain't coming to Thanksgiving dinner."

"That's a good point." Mark took a sip from Paul's Thermos.

Their ears perked up at the sound of tree limbs snapping. Paul steadied his rifle. A small doe emerged and walked toward the corn and fed. Paul sighed, and sat back.

"We ain't gonna shoot it?" Mark asked.

"That's not what we came here for."

"Well at least we'd go home with something. If I go home empty handed to Charlene, she's gonna hit me with a fry pan."

Paul sighed, and he knew for once his idiot cousin was right. They'd been in the woods for over 14 hours. The thought of leaving empty-handed just didn't feel right. He motioned for Mark to take the shot.

The rifle cracked and the deer dropped. A perfect shot painlessly ended the doe's existence. They climbed down from the stand and walked toward the fallen animal.

"Heck of a shot," Paul said, clapping his cousin on the back. The marksman smiled.

"She's a fat little doe." Mark knelt and inspected the kill. "Figure we'll just toss her in the back of the truck and dress her when we get home. Too dark now and I don't want some mountain cat smelling the blood and trying to get a free meal."

"Can't argue with that. I'll help you carry her."

Paul stooped to cradle the doe's hind legs when a glint of light caught his eye. Mark picked up his half just as Paul let go, and the deer crashed to the ground.

"What the heck, Paul?" Mark shot. "I could've pulled out my back."

"Just look," Paul said, motioning for Mark to keep his voice down and pointing toward a line of trees.

"Look at what? All I see is darkness and . . . oh."

A gold hue swirled around a cluster of trees. The massive head of the stag poked out and stared at the two hunters. It was glorious, almost angelic in its appearance. The deer rounded a tree and peered at the hunters through massive eyes that resembled inky pools. It took a few steps to the side, and its body moved as if it were one single fluid organism. It *danced.*

"Well would you look at that?" Mark asked. "It's real."

He yelped as the rifle shot boomed in the night air. The stag reared back and fled, weaving through the trees. Mark turned and saw the smoking gun in Paul's hands.

"Now what'd you do that for? You missed him anyway."

"Like hell I did. Hit him right in the flank. That deer is hobbled and we should be able to track him. Come on."

They left the doe and ran to where the stag appeared. Paul removed his flashlight and scanned the foliage, looking for a slick patch they could follow.

"Oh man, check this out." Mark raised his hand, and Paul shone the light on it.

His hand was coated with a thick, green sludge that Paul assumed had to be the deer's blood. It was far from normal, but when dealing with a deer that shone like the sun, normal was out the window.

"Now what in the heck is that?"

Mark brought his hand to his mouth and licked it. Paul retched at the thought.

"Sure tastes like blood to me." Mark wiped the sludge hand on his shirt.

Paul shook his head and shone the light on the ground. Green splotches and deer tracks created a trail for them to follow. They walked for several minutes and Paul expected to find the animal resting on its side, waiting its death like any normal deer would. Frustration set in as the tracks vanished and the blood dried up.

"That's one tough deer," Paul said.

The golden stag snorted, its body hidden behind

a tree line. Paul almost dropped his gun, and Mark nearly yelled in surprise. The deer took off as soon as it was spotted. The cousins gave chase. It would lose them for a few minutes, and then reappear as if taunting them, daring them to try and catch it.

"I don't like this. Doesn't feel right."

"Shut up, Mark. That deer is smart and hell, probably old as these woods, but a well-placed shot will bring it down. It'll fall, and then we'll be famous."

They tracked the deer until the woods started to break and clear out, revealing the side of a mountain neither had seen before. Large holes were cut into the side, and the area was silent and devoid of life. It was like the forest just stopped in its tracks.

"Think it went inside one of those caves?" Mark pointed to the largest opening.

"Your guess is as good as mine."

They stepped into the clearing. Gold light shone from inside the larger cave. The deer strolled to the front and stood motionless. It dared one of the hunters to come for it. Paul and Mark inched closer and crouched, ready to send a barrage of bullets into the animal. Just as their fingers tickled the triggers, the deer was sucked back, as if yanked by an invisible rope.

"What the—?" Paul lowered his gun and Mark did the same.

A giant rush of hot wind blasted their faces. The pair fell back, choking on the foul stench. A rumble started from inside the cave and rocks tumbled from the side of the mountain. Paul's eyes went wide as the creature emerged.

It was massive, and the first thing they saw was the gaping mouth filled with jagged teeth. Three large tongues, slithering like snakes, darted from its gaping maw. Sinewy tendrils shot from all sides, suctioning it to the cave wall. It pulled itself forward, emitting a roar more chilling than a charging grizzly bear. It resembled a giant toad, its nose smashed in and yellow eyes sunk in deep pits. Above its head sat the golden stag, attached to the creature's head by a thin line of muscle. Paul saw it for what it truly was—a lure. The stag wasn't a mythical animal; only a part of a more magical and horrific entity used to lure food to its home.

"We need to go! Now!" Paul turned to flee when a barbed tongue shot like a whip and wrapped around his ankle, slamming him to the ground.

He dropped the gun and his chin struck the ground. The taste of warm blood filled his mouth, and tiny stars danced around his head. Mark screamed, but it sounded miles away.

He felt himself being dragged and knew it was toward that creature's greedy mouth. His hands scrabbled in the dirt. He clawed frantically trying to get free.

Mark stood there, frozen in shock.

"Mark! Help me, please!"

Mark snapped out of his trance and ran toward his cousin, grabbing Paul's arms and pulling back with all the strength in him. They were both dragged to the cave opening. Mark reached into his pocket and secured the knife, handing it to his cousin. Paul then desperately slashed at the thick, black muscle. The creature uttered a cry of defiance and inched further from inside the cave. Another barbed tongue shot from its mouth and whipped past Mark's head. He retreated back.

"Jesus, no! Don't leave me to die like this," Paul begged

"I ain't leaving you cuz. I'm improvising."

Mark ran to where his gun had fallen and steadied the rifle, taking aim. He took a deep breath and pulled the trigger, sending a shot right through one of the creature's yellow eyes. The monster howled in agony and thrashed about as the eye exploded. Thick green blood poured from it like a broken dam. A clawed hand emerged from its side and gripped the damaged eye. Paul felt the tongue loosen and kicked free, fumbling to his feet and stumbling toward the safety of the woods.

"Come on, Mark. Let's get out of here." He grabbed his cousin's shirt as he passed and the pair took off, crashing through shrubs and trampling any plants in their way.

They ran until their legs wobbled and their lungs burned. Satisfied with the distance they'd put between themselves and the monster, Paul collapsed against a tree and Mark sat on a fallen trunk.

They looked at one another, unsure what to say next or what could even be said.

"Reckon we ought to get that doe before a cougar runs off with it?" Mark said.

"Yeah, I think that'd be a good idea right about now. I think this is going to be my last hunt for quite a while."

The cousins walked together to where the doe would be waiting for them to bring home. They vowed to take this unexpected hunt to their graves.

ABOUT THE AUTHORS

MARK C. SCIONEAUX is a Bram Stoker Award nominated editor and author.

He is the author of numerous short stories appearing in various anthologies. He is also the author of *FAMILY DINNER*; and coauthor of *SLIPWAY GREY* and *CANNIBAL FAT CAMP*. *DIE, YOU ZOMBIE CRACKERS!* is the second release of the Splattire Series co-created with David C. Hayes.

A graduate of Louisiana State University, he currently resides in Baton Rouge, Louisiana with his wife, Jessica.

DAVID C. HAYES is an award-winning author, editor and filmmaker. Most recently, he has written stories for Dark Moon Books, Strangehouse Books, Evil Jester Press, Blood Bound Books and many more. His first collection, *American Guignol*, was released in 2013 and he is a multiple genre anthology editor. He is the author of *Cannibal Fat Camp, Muddled Mind: The Complete Works of Ed Wood Jr., Cherub* (also from Bizarro Pulp Press) and the *Rottentail* graphic novel as well as many screenplays, stage plays (his *Dial P for Peanuts* won an Ethingtony in 2011), articles and more.

His films, like *The Frankenstein Syndrome, Bloody Bloody Bible Camp, A Man Called Nereus, Dark Places* and *Back Woods*, are available worldwide. He is the co-owner of Cinema Head Cheese (www.cinemaheadcheese.com), a geek culture website, and you can visit him online at www.davidchayes.com. David is a voting member of the Horror Writers Association and the Dramatists Guild. He likes creepy hugs and all kinds of cheese.

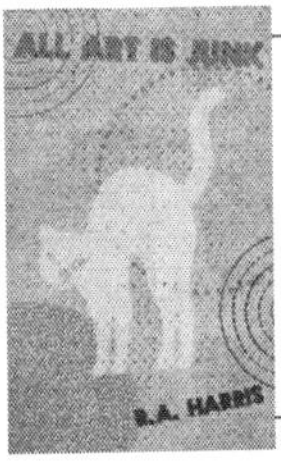

All Art is Junk by R. A. Harris

Lana Rivers, a girl with paintbrush hair, is missing and it's up to Lancelot, her cyborg knight, and his bionic conjoined twin, Cilia, to find her before her evil father, a disrespected artist turned mad-scientist, performs a terrible experiment on her.

Cherub by David C. Hayes

Cherub wasn't like the other boys—too slow, too rough—but he didn't deserve what that hospital did to him, and now he will make them pay.

Skinners by Adam Millard

Los Angeles, the City of Angels. At least, that's what the brochure says. What it fails to mention is the earthquakes. Oh, and the flesh-eating creatures lying dormant beneath the concrete, waiting for the chance to surface once again. Their wait is over . . .

The After-Life Story of Pork Knuckles Malone by MP Johnson

What's a farm boy to do when his pet pig becomes an evil, decaying hunk of ham with slime-spewing psychic powers?

A Lightbulb's Lament by Grant Wamack

A gentleman with a lightbulb for head wakes up in a world full of darkness, hooks up with a beautiful ex-prostitute, and an old man who can heal people; he travels down south to find the mysterious Creator.

The Horror Show by Vincenzo Bilof

A poetry novel—a narcoleptic, amnesiac Nobel Prize-winning poet becomes the subject of an experiment to cure madness.

Gravity Comics Massacre by Vincenzo Bilof

An absolutely shitty novella involving comic books, aliens, a serial killer, teenagers in an abandoned town, horror-trope dream sequences, and an ending you're going to hate.

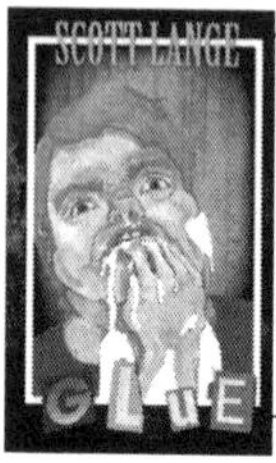

Glue by Scott Lange

Sticky bowels and sticky situations.

Ascent by Matthew Bialer

Is the 8 foot tall creature haunting a small town in Iowa in the fall of the year 1903 the product of a hoax and collective imagination or was it one of the first documented paranormal event in America? This epic poem grapples with these questions.

Fecal Terror by David Bernstein

A killer turd is on the loose!

Cucumber Punk by P. A. Douglas

Cucumbers, punks, and lumber. What's not to love?

Terence, Mephisto & Viscera Eyes by Chris Kelso

9 new science fiction stories from Chris Kelso

Bizarro Bizarro: An Anthology

The finest bizarro short stories from 2013.

Captain K and the Bearded Man Boy by P. A. Douglas

Pat is a super hero and his alcoholic dog can talk. The world must surely be ending.

Day of the Milkman by S. T. Cartledge

In a world dominated by the milk industry, only one milkman survives after a terrible storm sinks all the ships and throws the Great White Sea out of balance.

Moosejaw Frontier by Chris Kelso

An unapologetic disaster of metafiction

Notes from the Guts of a Hippo by Grant Wamack

A rugged journalist travels to Brazil in search of a missing hippo researcher and the notes left behind lead to something earth shatteringly revelatory.

Industrial Carpet Drag by Bruce Taylor

Chemicals make you do great things!

29713535R00110

Made in the USA
Middletown, DE
29 February 2016